Dear America

A Line in the Sand

★ ★ ★

The Alamo Diary of Lucinda Lawrence

BY SHERRY GARLAND

Scholastic Inc. New York

Gonzales, Texas
1835

★ ★ ★

Wednesday, September 9, 1835

First thing I did upon awakening this morning was smell my new cedar pencils and the cover of my new diary. I still cannot believe they are mine. They arrived yesterday with the supplies, a gift from my dear Grandmother Lawrence in Missouri in honor of my thirteenth birthday.

I was engaged in school lessons at Mrs. Roe's house when I heard the ruckus — the entire populace of little Gonzales spilling out of log cabins into the muddy street to greet the creaky supply wagons rolling up from the Guadalupe River ferry. All the Texas colonies are far removed from civilization, but our DeWitt's Colony is the farthest west of them all. Supplies only come twice a year, by ship from New Orleans then overland by wagon.

I could hardly stand still as I watched the men unload barrels of molasses, flour, sugar, dried apples, pots, pans, churns, irons, barrels of whiskey, tobacco, coffee, dried beans, and other sundries. Mittie Roe almost swooned when she saw bolts of calico cloth and rolls of silk ribbon. She hankers after hair ribbons more than any girl I know. I suppose it's because she has such pretty, fine hair. The fanciest ribbon in the world wouldn't help my coarse red hair. Mama says it looks like a horse's tail.

The supply ship also brought mail from the States. My little brother, Green, ran to the fields to fetch Papa, Willis, and Lemuel, who were busy picking cotton. They dropped everything, for the arrival of supplies and mail is almost as grand an occasion as Christmas or the Fourth of July. Besides my diary, Grandmother Lawrence's package included some milled blue cloth. The sight almost brought tears to Mama's eyes and she ran her calloused fingers over the cloth as if it were a silk wedding dress.

I hear the whippoorwills in the woods. The summer heat is still with us, so my three brothers are asleep on pallets in the breezy dogtrot between the two rooms of the log cabin. I am here in the dark room lit by a candle that casts dancing shadows across the walls. Mama has washed Papa's feet in the wash pan and told me to snuff out the flame. My mind spins with thoughts of what to record in my diary, but for now I will hide the pencils in a chink in the logs near my straw pallet. And I will hold the diary close to my heart all night long.

Thursday, September 10

Very early, before leaving for the cotton fields, Willis and Lemuel argued over a whittling knife that came in Grandmother's package. They both grabbed for it and got into an awful brawl until Papa ended the fight. He took the knife and turned right around and handed it to Green, who is but nine years old and has no need of a good whittling knife yet. Willis and Lem scowled, but dared not say one word to Papa about his system of discipline.

After supper tonight, Papa saw me writing in my new diary and said so much reading and writing can't be good for a girl and that I should pay more attention to my chores and learn how to sew and cook or else I won't get a good husband. Mama's back straightened and she clutched the iron poker. Says she, "Ain't nary a thirteen-year-old girl west of the Mississippi can sew straighter stitches or cook better than our Lucinda, Mr. Lawrence. Her chores is always done right proper. I don't reckon a bit of book learning will cause her harm."

When Papa saw the look on Mama's face he put his pipe down and said, "Why, I do believe Mrs. Lawrence is riled." Papa didn't say another word about my schooling after that.

Friday, September 11

Mrs. Roe received a slate board and a box of slate pencils in the supplies — they are the first I've ever seen. Mrs. Roe is Mama's second cousin and one of the few educated women in the colony. Most are like Mama, unable to read or write. Mrs. Roe teaches a few students in her house or under a live oak tree when it's hot. The older boys are all picking cotton now, so it's only me, Mittie, Green, and the younger Roe children. We have no money, for the cotton has not been sold yet. So we pay her with what we can — eggs, melons, or fresh honey that Lem finds in the woods.

Mittie's father, Thomas Roe, owns a broom-making shop and also makes furniture, but he is in Louisiana now, been gone for five weeks. Rumors say he ran off for good. Every time someone mentions him, Mittie clams up and changes the subject.

It's a mile walk from our farm to the Roe house on Water Street, but it's worth the trouble, for I love learning. And Mittie is my best friend. She is fourteen and knows more about fashions and parties than any girl in these parts. She taught me all the dance steps I know. She dragged me to the dance at the Fourth of July celebration and loaned me her best bonnet. Though, I must say, lately she has been acting peculiar. She used to be so much fun, always thinking up interesting things to do. But those rumors are bothering her.

Saturday, September 12

No lessons today. I saw Mittie coming down the path through the woods that passes behind Mama's vegetable garden full of pumpkins and melons and sweet potatoes. Mama says Mittie and I are as different as night and day. That's because I am tall as a pine tree and all legs. I'm always stumbling over my own big feet. My thick red hair hangs down my back in a single flat plait no matter what the occasion. Mittie is small and graceful as a swan. Her hair is the color of dark honey and she studies fashion plates in ladies' magazines to learn different ways to style her hair. Mittie sings like an angel; I can't carry a tune. And she would not be caught dead climbing a tree.

But Mama is wrong: Mittie and I do have some things in common. We both love flowers passionately and spend hours picking them, especially in the spring when the hills and prairies are blanketed with wildflowers every color of the rainbow. When I saw Mittie today she was carrying an armful of yellow sunflowers. I watched her place them at the memorial behind the smokehouse where there is a circle of stones and a wooden cross that marks the grave of my baby sister, Mary.

The grave is empty. Mary died of a fever in Mama's arms on our two-week voyage by schooner from New Orleans to Texas and was buried at sea. She was two years old. That journey was horrible. Mary was already sick from traveling down the Missouri River by flatboat, then down the Mississippi by steamboat. Green and I spent all our days and nights with our heads hung over the rail, retching into the Gulf of Mexico. We near starved and even Mama, as big-hipped as she is, looked like a scarecrow. First thing Papa did once we had staked our land and built our cabin was make the cross and arrange the stones as a memorial so Mama would have someplace to grieve. I can hardly recall what Mary looked like, but the sight of the cross keeps her in my thoughts most every day.

Sunday, September 13

Two more chickens were missing this morning, one our best laying hen. Lem says the footprints in the mud outside the barn belong to a panther.

The Sabbath is our only day of rest. Mama doesn't cook so we ate cold cornbread and cold ham for breakfast. Lem's pet raccoon, Bandit, got its paw chewed up in a trap, so he salved and bandaged it. Papa got mad, saying it was a waste of medicine needed for humans and livestock, not a useless critter like a raccoon. Lemuel took Bandit and hid up in a tall pecan tree, his favorite place when he gets fussed at by Papa. Lem is fifteen and a smidgen too old to be acting like that. Sometimes I think he is half critter himself. He stutters just like a squirrel when he tries to talk.

Papa's canvas sack is looking tattered, so he asked Mama to patch it. When he suggested she use the new blue cloth Grandmother Lawrence sent, Mama got boiling mad. Doesn't Papa know how precious a piece of cloth is to Mama? She hasn't had a new dress in a year and her bonnet is droopy. Every time we harvest cotton, Mama puts aside some to spin into thread and weave into rough homespun on Mrs. Roe's loom, but all that goes into making shirts for the menfolk or a dress for me. Poor Mama never has anything left for herself.

Monday, September 14

Washday. We're so low on lye soap, Mama is afraid we'll run out before hog-killing time. Papa has promised that he will render a couple of hogs as soon as the cotton's all been picked and the weather turns cold.

Green did the most disgusting thing today. While the water in the iron cauldron was boiling, before Mama had put in the soap and dirty clothes and stirred them with her paddle, Green tossed in a bullfrog. It hopped like crazy, but was dead and cooked before Mama could fish it out. I cried and Green laughed. Mama took a few swings at him, but he ducked and ran.

"Well, frog legs is eatable, you know," Mama said as she put the pitiful creature on a metal plate. "I reckon this will be Green's supper tonight." And it was. She made him eat those big ol' legs. He grinned and said they tasted better than chicken, but I don't think he'll do that again.

Tuesday, September 15

Ironed clothes and linens all day. I complained about having to constantly reheat our five irons in the fire, until Mama reminded me there are some who only have one iron. Papa's pants were intolerably wrinkled and I couldn't smooth them out, so Mama took over. Her arms are so strong, you can almost see the muscles through her sleeves. Mama decided to rip up some old mattress ticking to patch Papa's sack. I climbed up the ladder and got the old mattress down from the loft above the dogtrot.

My biggest fear in the world, besides Comanche raids and rattlesnakes, is black widow spiders, which have the nasty habit of hiding in what you store up there. Sure enough, when I shook out the mattress, two spiders ran across the floor. Green smashed them dead with his bare feet. What a little savage.

It is late evening, my favorite time. Just me and my diary. Everyone is asleep and the distant howling wolves sound so lonely. But I do not mind the solitude, for I have my thoughts to keep me company.

Wednesday, September 16

A man from San Felipe, in Austin's Colony, rode through town today. San Felipe is over a hundred miles northeast of here, on the Brazos River, and is the hub of the Texas colonies. It even has a printing press. The rider dropped off letters and a stack of the *Telegraph and Texas Register* newspaper. How I love reading those wrinkled, inky-smelling pages.

We received a letter from Mama's brother, Henry, who lives with his wife, Nancy, and five children in San Felipe. Uncle Henry has decided to move to DeWitt's Colony next spring. When Papa heard the news, he didn't say a word. He just walked out onto the gallery and washed his face. Papa's never admitted it out loud, but I don't think he likes Uncle Henry much. It's because of politics. Uncle Henry belongs to the War Party — he wants Texas to declare her independence from Mexico. Papa belongs to the Peace Party — he wants Texas to stay part of Mexico and urge a democratic constitution. Papa hates war. He says he saw enough killing in the War of 1812, serving under Andrew Jackson, who is now President of the United States.

Later that day —

After supper Papa looked up from the newspaper and said, "It's just a handful of slick lawyers and fool agitators causing all this talk about war. Most of the colonists are farmers like me who want to live their lives and raise their families and not get involved in politics."

Says Willis, "I've heard there are thirty thousand Americans settled in Texas now, and only four thousand Mexicans. If this were a democracy, the majority would rule. But this isn't America, it's Mexico, and Texians have no say in government affairs. That ain't right." Willis is just seventeen, but he talks like he knows everything.

Says Papa, "The Mexican army is one of the

biggest in the world. Even if the Texians fought a war and won, it would be a costly victory."

Willis jumped up from the table and said, "But, Papa, we can't just stand by and give up our freedoms. Grandpa Lawrence fought in the American Revolution, didn't he? And you fought the British at Horseshoe Bend. When it comes my time to fight for freedom, I'll not turn my back."

Papa shook his head as Willis left the room. Mama looked up from poking the fire logs and said, "Now, don't those words sound mighty familiar, Mr. Lawrence? I recollect you getting all fired up twenty-nigh years ago and running off to join the Georgia volunteers."

Papa snorted, then got quiet, lost in his memories.

Thursday, September 17

Talk of war has been going on all summer. Sometimes it scares me, but I think it is just talk. I don't believe war will really come. We are American born, but now we are Mexican citizens, for Texas is part of the Republic of Mexico. We came for the fertile, cheap land and the chance to farm and make a decent living.

Those early times were hard; some gave up, but not Papa. He says our roots are sunk too deep into Texas soil to pull up now. I think the worst is behind us and only good looms on the horizon. Our cotton crop is the grandest we've ever had, the town is growing, and a schoolhouse is to be built next spring. And the land is so unspoiled and beautiful — sometimes my heart fills up with so much joy and freedom, I have to whoop and run across the prairie like a wild mustang. I pray we never, never leave this place.

Friday, September 18

Lem came in toting an oozing slab of golden honeycomb. I carried a crock full of the honey to Mrs. Roe as payment for school lessons. She was sewing Mittie a new dress, made from one of her old ones. That makes four for Mittie. I only have two dresses and both are plain as dirt. Of a sudden Mittie hands me a blue bundle and says, "I thought you might want this old dress of mine. Your mama can make you a skirt or a shirt for Green from it."

My mouth dropped when I saw the familiar dress and I cried out, "But, Mittie, it's the blue calico — your papa's favorite. He always says you look pretty as a blue flower, remember?" I pushed the dress back into her hands.

"Well, Papa isn't ever going to see it again, is he?" She

threw the dress on the floor, then burst into tears and climbed up the ladder to the top floor where she sleeps. I must remember not to mention her father again.

After supper tonight, Papa said he would take the day off tomorrow to cut some trees in the woods so the logs will be cured by the time Uncle Henry arrives in the spring. We will have a house raising then and, afterwards, food and music and dancing — it is about the only amusement we ever have.

Saturday, September 19

A horrible, horrible day. My fingers still tremble as I write. Papa drove to the woods to cut logs for Uncle Henry's cabin. Willis was off hunting geese with his best friend, Galba Fuqua. Around noon, as Green and I took Papa his lunch, we heard an awful scream. I thought it was Indians, but next thing I knew, a panther leaped at the ox. The ox went crazy and knocked Papa to the ground, then thrashed around. The reins wrapped around Papa and pinned him against a tree.

Green ran to get Mama and Lem. The ox was so scared and confused, suddenly it turned on Papa and gored him in his thigh and side. It made me sick to see Papa's blood coming through his pants and shirt.

I was about to club the ox on the head with a tree

limb when I heard Mama shout for me to step aside. I turned and saw her aiming Papa's old Kentucky rifle. A loud boom shook the air, and smoke and fire spat out of the barrel. The ox dropped to its knees, then keeled over, trembling in pain. Mama reloaded the gun and shot the poor animal dead to put it out of its misery. We cut the reins with Green's new whittling knife. Willis and Galba, having heard the shots, ran up and helped us get Papa to the house.

I stood in the yard while Dr. Pollard cut off Papa's pants and shirt and washed the wounds, then wrapped them up. Papa shouted with pain. Mama told me and Green to fetch more water for the kettle over the hearth and then she told Willis and Lem to slaughter the ox and bring the meat to the house as there was no point in wasting beef. Lem said if Papa died, he was not going to eat one bite of the beef no matter how hungry he was.

It's late now and my brothers are snoring like it has been an ordinary day. Mama is still awake, sitting beside Papa, washing his face. His fever is fierce and the doctor says the next few days will determine if he lives or dies.

★ ★ ★

Sunday, September 20

Papa's fever is still high and he cries out "Cotton! Cotton!" in his delirium. Mama did not sleep all night. Her eyes are swollen and lined with dark circles. I milked the cow and gathered eggs, then cooked breakfast. Mama didn't eat more than two bites but drank a whole pot of coffee. My brothers gave up their coffee for her; I thought that was sweet of them.

Mama asked me to read the latest newspaper aloud to Papa, though he is unconscious. The *Telegraph and Texas Register* is full of talk of war. The Mexican president, General Antonio López de Santa Anna, has declared all Texian dissidents to be traitors to Mexico and vows to drive out all those squatters who have come to Texas illegally — thousands of them. Texian settlements are forming militias to protect the colonists from Mexican soldiers.

While I read, Mama sat in the rocking chair and fell asleep. How I wished Papa would snort or grumble when I read about the young lawyer, William Travis, who had agitated the Mexicans back in June at Anahuac. That ruckus almost caused a war right then and there. But Papa is quiet, except for heavy, painful breathing. The wet rag has slipped from his forehead. I must put this diary aside and get more water from the bucket.

Monday, September 21

Papa's fever broke this eve. I was reading about some Texians who captured a Mexican schooner sent to collect duties. Papa blinked and said, "Galderned fools gonna get us all kilt." I threw my arms around him and made so much commotion, Mama woke up and jumped out of her rocking chair. The rocker caught the cat by the tail and you never heard such a racket. My brothers all came running up to the bed like they were ready to fight Comanche. The hound dogs commenced to yelping, the pigs under the house commenced to squealing, and the mules commenced to braying until you'd think it was the end of the world. Papa said, "What in thunderation is all that racket, Mrs. Lawrence?" and Mama said, "It's your welcoming committee, Mr. Lawrence," then she smiled.

Tuesday, September 22

After supper, before the mosquitoes got bad, we helped Papa out to the front porch and I read more of the newspaper to all. Mama rocked and sewed, Papa smoked his pipe, and the boys whittled. At that moment I don't think Papa was sorry I knew how to read and write. I was reading an editorial about how cruel and unjust General Santa Anna is, when Green suddenly barked out, "Why does everybody hate ol' Santy Anna so much, anyhow?"

Willis stood and says, "He's a dictator, that's why." Then Willis explained all the grievances that the Texians had against Santa Anna, like abolishing the Constitution of 1824, and sending soldiers to collect taxes.

After Willis finished, Papa laughed and says, "Maybe if the Texians would obey the laws they said they would, the Mexican government wouldn't have to send soldiers here."

Every time Willis named a complaint, Papa had an excuse for Mexico. Pretty soon Willis got flustered. His face turned red and he ran his fingers through his mop of rusty hair. He drew in a deep breath, then says, "Well, ol' General Santa Anna lives like a king and wastes everybody's tax money. He has a saddle of gold and I hear he has a sword that cost seven thousand dollars — why, you could buy half of Texas for that. They say when he's on a war campaign, he sleeps in a silk tent and drinks from a fancy silver teapot with fancy china, while his men eat beans. Brings young women into his tent, though he's got a wife back in Veracruz. Brings along roosters for cock fights every night and pays more for a single fighting rooster than a Texian pays for a horse. He's an opium addict. And — and — he uses a silver chamber pot!"

We busted out laughing, even Mama who doesn't allow such talk in the house. Papa laughed so hard his eyes teared up. "You've got me there, son. Now, there's a good reason if I ever heard one for going to war — the man uses a silver chamber pot."

Wednesday, September 23

Willis's friend Galba came over for supper. He is sixteen and so very fine and handsome. My heart pounds like a drum whenever he comes near, but he thinks of me like a little sister. He yanked my pigtail, then made faces while I was reading the last of the newspaper. I giggled until Papa shot a glance that wilted my toes.

I read that Santa Anna had sent soldiers to San Antonio de Bexar, a Mexican town about seventy-five miles east of here, and had garrisoned them in an old Spanish mission called the Alamo. Mama had a worried look. Her youngest brother, Isaac, lives in San Antonio where he owns a store. His pretty wife,

Esperanza, is expecting her first child in the spring. She is Mexican and extremely kind. She taught me some Spanish when I last saw her.

Lastly, I read that Stephen F. Austin, a Peace Party leader and the most respected man in Texas, had been released after almost two years of unjust imprisonment in a Mexican jail. Mr. Austin was the first man to bring American settlers into Texas. Over one thousand attended a party in his honor. I'll bet it was a grand thing to see! If we do not have a party soon, I am afraid I will forget all the dance steps Mittie taught me.

Mr. Austin, who has always believed in strictly obeying the laws in Mexico, now vows that war is the only recourse. There is to be a convention in San Felipe in mid-October with representatives sent from all the major settlements.

"Well, it's about time Austin came to his senses," Galba said. "I'm sick of Santa Anna and his dictator ways. 'Fore you know it, we'll all be his slaves."

Papa tapped his pipe on the porch rail loudly. Galba got quiet, then put on his hat and said he had to go. Willis left with him. Papa stood up and muttered, "Dern fool agitators are gonna get us all kilt. Those causing the biggest stink don't live seventy-five miles from the Mexicans like we do. They have two or three rivers twixt them and the soldiers at San Antonio. If war comes, Gonzales will be the first town to burn." Papa's words chilled my soul; even now I cannot get them out of my mind.

Thursday, September 24

Cotton, cotton, how I hate picking cotton. Last night Willis and Lem complained that they could not possibly pick all the cotton by themselves, with Papa being too hurt to work, so Mama volunteered herself, me, and Green. We worked from dawn until afternoon, then me and Mama left to cook supper. My fingers are pricked and bleeding from hitting the sharp brown hulls. Some folks pull the boll, hull and all. It's faster, but picked cotton gets a higher price.

Friday, September 25

This afternoon after picking, Willis saw my hands and shouted, "Sweet Jericho! You look like you've been chewed by a bear. I'm going to march you to town and buy some ointment and get you some gloves." When I asked him where he was going to get the money, he just said, "Never you mind."

We went to Miller's general store and I heard Willis negotiating to do work in exchange for the ointment.

I was looking at gloves when suddenly Green came running down the street, blithering like an idiot and shouting to everyone he saw.

"Mexican soldiers! Across the river. They've got guns."

Men dropped what they were doing, grabbed their rifles, and hurried to the river, with women and children following behind. I saw four Mexican soldiers in bright red-and-blue uniforms, an oxcart, and a driver. The Mexican leader ordered Andrew Ponton, who is the *alcalde*, our town's mayor, to send the ferry across the river, but he refused. So a soldier had to swim the river with a written message.

Word spread like wildfire that the message was from the Mexican general at San Antonio. He was requesting that Gonzales return the little six-pounder cannon that Mexico had loaned us four years ago as protection during Indian attacks. Everyone in Gonzales knows the little cannon is broken and useless as a weapon of war, but it makes a boom that scares off the Comanche.

The *alcalde* called an emergency meeting, and the town council decided it best for the men to get the women and children safely out of town, then come back and fight, if necessary. The *alcalde* dispatched messengers to spread the word to the rest of the Texian settlements and to ask for volunteers to come to our aid. Eighteen men agreed to stay behind and guard the ferry.

As we headed home, Green grabbed my sleeve and said, "Are the Mexicans going to kill us all?"

Willis said, "Don't worry, our eighteen men against their five is pretty good odds." His words reassured Green, but I must say pretty soon the town was bustling with so much activity and panic that it was hard to stay calm.

Later —

When we told Papa what was happening, he knotted his eyebrows and says, "That little six-pounder? Why, it can't even shoot a cannonball, even if we had one to load in it."

Willis crammed his hat on his head and says, "Santa Anna doesn't really need that cannon, he just doesn't want us to have any weapons. This is the beginning of disarming the colonies. If we give up the cannon, next thing you know, Santa Anna will want our hunting rifles, then our pistols, then our Bowie knives, then our whittling knives."

Green gasped. "Old Santy Anna ain't gonna get my

new whittling knife." He took it out of his pocket and headed toward the door, shouting, "I'm fixing to bury my knife just like they're burying the cannon in Mr. Davis's peach orchard."

The words were hardly out of Green's mouth when Mittie Roe came running up. "We're heading for the river bottom where it'll be safer. The Mexican army is on its way! Ma says can she drive our wagon alongside yours?"

"Five soldiers is hardly the Mexican army," Papa said, but Mittie stood her ground. Says she, "All the town's leaving for the woods and river bottoms. There's gonna be a scrape for sure. The *alcalde* says we'll never surrender up that cannon. If the general wants it, he'll have to come and take it."

Mama's eyes clouded with worry, but she turned back to Papa. "I don't imagine the Mexicans will care about an old woman like me. I'll stay here with Mr. Lawrence. But Cinda, you pack up some food for yourself and your brothers. Lem, take the milk cow and her calf. Willis, hitch up the mules to the wagon. Ride alongside the Roes and watch over them." Nobody argues with Mama when she has that tone of voice.

★ ★ ★

Saturday, September 26

I packed cold cornbread, ham, and five baked potatoes that had been cooking in hot coals all night. Mama loaded her most prized possessions onto the wagon — a mantel clock, her best quilts, and her spinning wheel. Lemuel put a lead rope on the cow, and her calf followed behind bawling pitifully. Willis cleaned the Kentucky rifle and filled his powder horn. Papa loaded his pistol.

Just before we left, Mama took me aside. Her chin quivered, but she wasn't crying as she tied my bonnet strap. She said, "Be strong, Cinda. Watch over Green. If anything happens to me and Papa, you'll be the woman of the family. Raise him right." She hugged me tight. It was not until that moment that I realized I might never see her or Papa again. Panic filled my heart. Try as I might, I couldn't stop the tears from filling my eyes. I wanted to stay with Mama, but I had to be strong, so I took Green by the hand and put him in the wagon.

I think Willis would have rather been guarding the ferry than taking care of women and children, but he took his responsibility and watched over us like a mother hen. Our wagon reached the woods before sunset.

We are now camped within sight of the Guadalupe River, several miles upstream from the town. The ground is wet from a recent rain and we are devoured by mosquitoes. Every inch of exposed flesh is an itching eruption of bumps. Mittie's youngest sister, Permelia, cries and scratches endlessly.

It is almost dark, so I must close. We can't make a fire because the Mexicans might see us. I wish Mittie could sleep in our wagon, but she must help watch over the children. I know I will not sleep. The mosquitoes, the hoot owls, the wind moaning, the wolves, and the thought of snakes slithering into our camp will make it impossible for me to close my eyes. I cannot bear to think of Mama and Papa all alone.

Sunday, September 27

It does not seem like Sunday without Mama here. Every Sunday I comb her long red hair that reaches the floor and after she twists it up on her head, we go on the front porch and I read from the Bible. Usually the Roes come over and we sing hymns.

This morning, after breakfast, Mrs. Roe got out her Bible. Says she, "I hear that a traveling Methodist preacher is in the area. I reckon he'll rake in a bushel of sinners like he did at the last camp revival. Lordy, those

Methodists do get all fired up." We all laughed, for we are Baptists.

That revival was two years ago. Just about every child old enough to walk lined up and got baptized in the icy Guadalupe River. Folks came from farms and far out settlements and camped out for three days. Men killed beeves and women barbecued them out under the oak trees. Folks ate and sang and clapped and played fiddles and repented and I must confess there were a few bottles of corn liquor being passed behind the bushes.

Protestant ministers are not supposed to preach in Mexican territory. All the American colonists who came to Texas swore to become Catholics, but I've only seen a Catholic priest once in five years. He performed marriages and baptized anyone who was not a Catholic. So I got sprinkled by the Catholics to please the Mexican government and dunked by the Protestants to please Mama. I suppose my soul is in good shape now.

Monday, September 28

Mittie and I walked to the river for water, and she swore she saw an Indian or a Mexican soldier behind every bush, and we jumped at every little noise. Finally she said, "Let's sing hymns to take our minds off our worries." Mittie has the loveliest voice on earth. I didn't feel like singing, but I agreed, for I knew it would lift her spirits. Later, Lem told me our voices carried through the woods and if the Mexicans didn't know where we were before, they surely did now. I didn't have the heart to tell Mittie what he said. Two other families joined us today, thank the Lord.

Willis says if there is no word by morning, he will return to town and investigate. Lemuel saw some honeybees and took off. When he came back, he had a leather pouch filled with honeycomb. Bandit, the raccoon, was sitting on his shoulder, licking his sticky paws. Mrs. Roe is giving us school lessons to pass the time. I memorized a sonnet.

Oh, these mosquitoes are feasting again. Papa told me once that Karankawa Indians smear alligator grease over their bodies to keep away mosquitoes. Smelly though it is, I understand why, if it keeps those flying demons away. How I miss my bed and the warm fire. Most of all I miss Mama and Papa.

Tuesday, September 29

Right after sunrise, we heard loud hoofbeats. It was Texians from settlements north and east of here on their way to help Gonzales. Familiar Gonzales men were also returning after getting their families to safety. Willis whooped and said he was going to join them, for he figured there was going to be a big scrape and he didn't want to be left out. Lem, who has no stomach for fighting and killing, said he would stay and watch over me and Green. Willis thanked him sincerely and told us not to return to town until all was clear. There is a little fort there, but we rarely use it anymore.

Men passed by all morning on their way to defend that pitiful cannon. When one big, bear-looking man rode by, Mrs. Roe says, "I guess those men will be rooting around for whatever food they can find in our houses and gardens." Another woman sighed and says, "Well, there goes my potato patch." Then Mittie says, "There goes the hen eggs." Then another one says, "There goes my snuff. I knowed I should have brung it with me." We all laughed our heads off.

I wonder if Papa is out of bed yet. I hope he doesn't do anything foolish. Just before we left, he tried to stand up and reopened his wound, bloodying his shirt. Papa is one of the best marksmen in the colony. He'll defend Mama with his last drop of blood. But I pray he won't have to.

Wednesday, September 30

I write hastily by the light of the moon as I sit in the back of the wagon. Lemuel snuck off at dawn to find out what was going on in town. When he came back, thrashing through the bushes, it was a miracle that Mrs. Roe didn't clobber him with her ax.

Lem reported that on Monday the Texians had crossed the river and captured four of the five Mexicans. Tuesday, a Mexican lieutenant showed up across the river with one hundred dragoons. The ferry and all boats are on this side, so they couldn't get across. The lieutenant asked for an interview with the *alcalde,* but the eighteen men guarding the ferry informed him Mr. Ponton was out of town. Wednesday, some townsmen finally met with the Mexicans and explained we weren't going to give up that cannon because it was needed for protection from the Indians. The Mexicans left. Lem figures they are going up the river to look for a shallow place to ford, and then coming back toward town on this side. And we're right in their path!

At that news, Mittie gasped and Mrs. Roe's face turned white. Lem broke up camp and we are headed back home. We figure it's safer there than in the woods. I can't wait to see Mama and Papa.

Thursday, October 1

We arrived back in Gonzales today. Such bustling and activity! About two hundred Texian men from nearby colonies are in town preparing to fight. They dug up the cannon from the peach orchard and the black-smith, Almeron Dickinson, took charge of it. There was no coal, so Green and some boys burned wood into charcoal for the gunsmith. After they repaired the cannon as best they could, they mounted it on the axles of a cotton wagon. Other men prepared shot by cutting up pieces of chain and melting down any iron they could find to form rough cannonballs.

I saw the widow DeWitt, whose late husband Green DeWitt was the founder of our colony. She was carrying a piece of white cloth in her arms, which she handed to the commander of the Texians. He unfurled a six-foot white flag. In the middle of the flag was a replica of the little cannon, with a single black star above it, and the words "Come and Take It" written below.

"We made it from my daughter Naomi's wedding dress," Mrs. DeWitt explained. Everyone cheered at the beautiful flag.

When I got home I hugged Mama and kissed Papa and bawled my eyes out and swore I would never,

never be separated from them again. Uncle Henry had arrived with the Texian volunteers from San Felipe and though Mama was glad to see him, I could tell that she was worried.

Mama and I cooked enough food for three days and packed knapsacks for Willis and Uncle Henry. Though Papa doesn't like fighting, he didn't say a word of protest. I was too nervous to eat.

This evening, about one hundred and fifty Texians crossed the river by ferry. They decided they would not wait for Mexican soldiers to attack Gonzales, but would find them and attack first. With heavy hearts we said farewell to Willis and Uncle Henry. I think every woman was silently weeping, though we cheered and tried to show courage and act like ladies. It is eerily quiet now. After she fed Papa, I saw Mama go behind the smokehouse to Baby Mary's grave. That is where she always goes to be alone with her thoughts and to have a good cry.

Friday, October 2

Land o' Goshen! The battle is on! It is just past day-break and the fog is thick in the woods and hovers over the river. We were awakened by the most awful shriek. Nothing can describe it. Then came the *pop*, *pop*, *pop* of rifles in the distance. Papa says the scream is the old six-pounder cannon. Lord Almighty! No wonder the Indians are afraid of it!

The noise has stopped, and I am seizing the moment to make my diary entry. Who knows when I will have the opportunity again. If the Texians lose this fight, I may be in my grave this time tomorrow. Oh, the shooting and noise have started up again. My heart is pounding like a drum. Lord protect us.

The noise has been over for two hours now. I was worried sick, but a messenger just arrived with news that the victory is ours and the Mexican dragoons are on the run back to San Antonio. I am delirious with relief. I've never heard such laughing and cheering. There is to be a fandango tonight to celebrate. Some men have gone to round up beeves to barbecue.

It is one o'clock in the morning now and still the fiddles play "Turkey in the Straw," "Molly Cottontail," and "Piney Woods" while the Texians dance in the middle of the street. Mama made me leave the fandango about midnight, saying it isn't proper for a thirteen-year-old girl to be in the company of such rowdy men who've been drinking liquor all night.

I am furious with Mittie. I cannot even bear to write what she did, so I will blow out the candle and try to sleep, though the noise of the fiddle comes through the window.

I left my bonnet someplace.

Saturday, October 3

I walked to town to look for my bonnet. The fandango lasted until daybreak and drunk men were sleeping on the ground and on porches.

I vowed I would not speak to Mittie today if I saw her. After the way she acted last night, I may never speak to her again. She knows I have had a fancy for Galba since I came to Texas. There was no shortage of men at the fandango last night, being about two hundred men and hardly fifty women, so Mittie could have picked on someone else.

How I love the Virginia reel and the cotillion and the waltz. Uncle Henry is an excellent dancer and he swirled me around like I was a rag mop. I danced with Willis a time or two, until he worked up the courage to ask some girls his own age to dance. And Lem would rather be off in the woods with the raccoons than at a dance.

I watched Galba all night long, praying he would ask me to dance and wondering if I dared to ask him. By midnight, when the music started up for what would be my last dance, I mustered up courage to walk up to Galba. But before I could speak, Mittie grabbed his arm and said, "You promised me a dance and I'm claiming it now."

I was so horrified I broke into tears and cried all the way home. Lem followed after me, saying, "What's g-got your g-goat?" and I said Mittie stole my beau, and Lem said, "M-Mittie is f-fourteen. You'll have to w-wait another year or t-two before you t-try to s-snare a b-beau."

I don't care if Mittie is older than me, she is supposed to be my friend. I never would have done that to her.

Sunday, October 4

All is excitement. More men keep arriving. Some are Texian farmers, others are Volunteers from the United States. They say broadsides are posted up all over the South, enticing men to join the Texas army in exchange for land. All the American newspapers are buzzing with news about Texas, getting Americans fired up. Papa says that President Andrew Jackson is itching to get Texas into the Union. Most of the Volunteers are young and untamed and looking for a big scrape. Papa wishes they would all stay home and mind their own business, but I think fighting for freedom is a noble cause. Rumors say there will be a Texas army uniform; how dashing the young men will look.

We ran out of cornmeal, so though it is the Sabbath, I spent all morning outside grinding corn in our little steel mill. It's a fine tool and is Papa's most prized possession, but it makes such an awful racket a human can't hear a sound while grinding. Every time I stopped to pour more dry corn down the funnel, my ears would ring. At the rate the Volunteers are eating our food, we'll all be skeletons by Christmas.

Monday, October 5

Uncle Henry is staying with us now. He feels to blame for Papa's accident since Papa was cutting logs for his house when he got gored. This morning Uncle Henry killed a wild pig and brought it to the house, but

Papa was too proud to take it and said his sons were perfectly capable of providing meat for the family while he was laid up. He made Willis take the pork to the Volunteers camped in a cornfield outside town. Mama didn't say anything to Papa, but she slammed pots and pans around the hearth for most of the morning.

Tuesday, October 6

A courier rode into town today with some frightful news. The Mexican general in San Antonio, the one who had demanded the little cannon, is believed to be on his way to Gonzales with five hundred soldiers and cannons.

About one hundred of the men decided to ride south of here to a little Spanish settlement called Goliad, in case the Mexicans come from that direction. There is an old Spanish presidio there, garrisoned by a few Mexican soldiers. Uncle Henry said he reckoned he would go with them. I know it is because he and Papa argue so much. Mama is so sad to see him go. She promised to watch over Aunt Nancy and the children if something happens to him.

★ ★ ★

Wednesday, October 7

Last night someone stole Uncle Henry's shirt that was hanging out to dry. Without a thought for himself, Willis gave Uncle Henry his best shirt. Mama took out the new blue cotton cloth and began sewing Willis a new one.

Thursday, October 8

Willis and I came across Mittie today at the river, sitting on a log, crying. Willis can always make her smile, so he sat beside her and tweaked her nose.

"What's wrong, did an alligator eat your bonnet?" he said.

Mittie tried to smile but choked on her tears. "Those awful boys won't stop teasing me about Papa. They say he ran off because he couldn't stand living with me and Mama and all the younguns. It isn't true. Papa *didn't* run off. I know he didn't."

Willis stopped joking and patted her shoulder. "Of course, he didn't run off. Why, I've heard that the rivers twixt here and Louisiana are higher than a pine tree. Your papa is just tied up waiting for his supplies. He'll be here before you know it, and all those boys will look like fools. Don't worry, I'll make sure they don't bother you anymore." He turned and headed toward town. When he passed by me he whispered, "Be kind to Mittie. She's upset over her pa."

I was still mad at Mittie because of the fandango, so I didn't want to talk. While I filled the water bucket, she picked an armful of yellow daisies. When we walked by the stones and wooden cross that mark Baby Mary's empty grave, Mittie handed me the flowers and said, "These are for little Mary." I couldn't stay mad at her after that. We pulled weeds from the grave and talked for an hour. She explained that she had grabbed Galba at the fandango because Willis teased her about not being able to dance, so she had to prove him wrong. We both laughed and hugged. I'm glad I don't have to be mad at her anymore.

Friday, October 9

There is no school and cotton picking has been delayed, for all the men think about is war. A messenger arrived in town with word that our boys had taken over the Spanish presidio in Goliad. Everyone is in high spirits now. Mama was relieved to hear that nobody got killed. The troops outside town bicker constantly, for no one can agree on who the leader will be. Papa says it sounds like they are the picture of disorganization.

Saturday, October 10

While at the general store, I met a tall, redheaded man with handsome features. He was buying ink and looking to purchase a new journal. He saw mine and admired it and told me he kept a daily journal, too. I told him it is my most prized possession. He smiled and said, "Good for you." Turns out that man was William Travis, the lawyer whose fiery speeches have been stirring things up in the colonies. He looked to be only about twenty-five or so.

Sunday, October 11

Just when it looked like this Texian army would never amount to a hill of beans, the most amazing thing happened — Mr. Stephen F. Austin himself rode into town. He is a slender man with dark wavy hair, a high intelligent forehead, and dark eyes. He wore a black suit that stood out among all the rough buckskin and homespun of most. He rode with great dignity.

Every man who saw him removed his hat and spoke with respect. And best of all, the grumbling and bickering stopped.

Though Mr. Austin has a bad cough and looks sickly and frail from the illness he caught while in prison, he was still unanimously elected to be the commander in chief of the army. He ordered supplies to be gathered and then organized the troops. They are to go east to San Antonio to face the Mexican soldiers garrisoned there. I cannot believe war is truly upon us. I did not think this day would ever come. I know freedom is a noble cause and our men must fight, but why is the lump in my throat so painful?

Monday, October 12

We are preparing for war. Willis and Lem cut down stalks of cane from the creek, ripped off the leaves, and attached old metal files to form poor man's lances. Willis asked me to strike a blow for freedom by making bullets. He showed me how to melt down every piece of lead I could find and pour the hot metal into hollow reeds. They are strange-looking bullets, but my heart swelled with pride when Willis said I did a fine job. Mama finished sewing his new shirt. She repaired the holes in his moccasins, too.

I cooked all the cornmeal we had, and boiled every egg I could find, and brought in beef from the smokehouse. We wrapped the food in Mama's tablecloth, then wrapped that with one of Mama's quilts. Willis put on his new shirt, then trimmed his hair. He never looked more handsome.

Poor Papa. His heart is breaking. He hates war, but he loves his son. Says Papa, "Son, do you think war is the answer?" Says Willis, "With five hundred Mexican soldiers on their way, it's the only recourse we have. We must fight for our rights and our families." Papa says, "Then go on. You're old enough to make your own decisions. Do what you think is right."

It is almost dark now. I hear the distant shouts of men across the river training for war. They will leave tomorrow. My heart aches that Willis will be among them, but I am proud of his courage and determination to fight for Texas's freedom. I must pray for our boys now, then try to sleep.

Tuesday, October 13

The Texian army left this morning for San Antonio. In the midst of the men was the little cannon on a makeshift cart whose wheels were made of big tree trunk circles. It squeaked and wobbled as two longhorn steers pulled it, Sarah DeWitt's "Come and Take It" flag waving proudly from a cane pole.

Every man, woman, and child lined the river and cheered as the army marched away. Boys climbed trees and women waved tear-stained handkerchiefs. Even Papa made us put him in the wagon and drive to the river, though his face grimaced with pain. As the men marched by, Papa said to a neighbor, "This coming war is like a boulder rolling down a mountain. If you can't stop it, best just get out of the way and let it do its damage."

From the poorest farmer to the wealthiest merchant, our brave men and boys marched off. My heart pounded as I saw Willis with Mama's colorful quilt rolled up on his back and the old Kentucky rifle and powder horn slung over his shoulder. He looked so serious and old.

Such a ragtag army! Some wore animal skin caps and buckskin breeches, stained with grease and dirt as if they had spent their lives in the woods. Others wore rough homespun linsey-woolsey. Some draped colorful Mexican *serapes* over their shoulders and wore Mexican *sombreros* on their heads; others wore plantation hats. I saw buffalo robes and store-bought blankets and quilts made by wives and mothers. Few leather boots were to be seen, but brogans and moccasins were plentiful. Spanish gourds and skin pouches served as water canteens.

Our little cannon bumped along beside them, smoke rising from the wooden wedge wheels, for the friction was great. It was their only piece of artillery, and a disabled one at that, to go against all the cannons of the Mexican army. For weapons, the men carried old muskets, long rifles, knives, or dueling pistols. They had no swords or bayonets, and Papa said there was hardly powder and lead enough between them to last a few days.

When a neighbor said to Papa, "They're all a bunch of fools," Green piped up, "They ain't fools, they're heroes."

The man laughed and said, "Same thing. Only difference twixt one and t'other is who wins the fight."

Then Green turned to Papa, all sad-eyed. "Papa, you would go if your leg wasn't hurt, wouldn't you?"

Papa watched the men filing by for a long time before lifting Green up into the wagon seat and wrapping one big arm around him. "Yes, I would go, Green. Not to fight, but to watch over Willis."

Heroes or fools, all I know is I never felt more proud to be a Texian.

★ ★ ★

Wednesday, October 14

The town is strangely quiet. Papa has spoken very little since the army left. Mittie and I went to the general store today to get some salt. We saw young Susanna Dickinson and her darling little girl, Angelina. The Dickinsons live a few cabins away from the Roes. Susanna's husband, Almeron, is the blacksmith in charge of the cannon.

Susanna asked me and Mittie to watch Angelina for a few minutes while she chopped some wood. Angelina has just learned to walk and is getting into everything. She is so pretty, with silky black hair and deep blue eyes; she looks much like her mother. Mittie and I let her walk back and forth between us and carried her piggyback around town until Susanna finished her work. Every time I see Angelina, I cannot help but think of Baby Mary and wonder how it would be to have a little sister.

I noticed that Susanna's eyes were red. She said she had got some lye soap in them, but Mittie and I are sure she was crying. She gave each of us a piece of sugarcane for our trouble. Sugar is about as rare as hen's teeth around here, so I chewed it slowly and crushed out the sweet juice. My tongue rejoiced.

Thursday, October 15

Papa said we could not delay picking the rest of the cotton another day or we will starve over the winter. We arrived at the cotton field at daybreak. The day started cold and miserable, but grew hot as we worked at a steady pace, dragging our long sacks behind us. Lem and I competed to see who could reach the end of our row first. None of us can top what Papa would have picked, close to three hundred pounds a day if his leg were healed. Mama and Lem pick under two hundred pounds, and I far less than that. But by the end of the day my full sack was so heavy I could hardly walk and every inch of my body ached.

The farmer across the river has much more land than Papa and owns slaves. We can hear the Negroes singing and chanting in deep, beautiful voices. Mama sings hymns to pass the time, but nothing makes the work easy.

Friday, October 16

Papa made himself a hickory walking stick and hobbles around the house and yard. My brothers are sleeping inside now, since the nights are getting right cool. That strange star in the evening sky seems bigger every night. Mrs. Roe says it is Halley's Comet. I sit on the porch and watch it each night. Some think it is an omen predicting terrible events. The sight of it frightens and awes me.

Tuesday, October 20

I have not written for three days because of picking cotton. My fingers got all pricked and sore. Each time I smeared on the ointment, I couldn't help but think of Willis. He worked at Miller's store many hours to pay for it. Thank the Lord, we finished picking cotton.

Lem drove the loaded wagon to the gin yesterday. From there, he took the bales to Dimitt's Landing on the Gulf where it will be sold and loaded on a ship for New Orleans. Lem was as excited as a puppy at the prospect of driving the wagon by himself. We gave him a list of supplies to buy with the money he receives. High on the list are blue shoes for me and new hats for Green and Papa.

Wednesday, October 21

Returned to school lessons today. Mittie almost wept when she saw my scratched-up hands. She said she wouldn't be caught dead picking cotton and she would rather starve than marry a farmer and work like a dog. I said, "Don't you mean a *poor* farmer?" She thought a minute, then said, "I suppose if I married a wealthy plantation owner, that would be satisfactory." We both laughed and made a secret vow to marry only rich farmers. Then we spent an hour talking about husbands and weddings. Mittie will have no trouble finding a husband, for she is pretty. But she worries about her small hips. Mama says she will have a hard time birthing children.

After lessons, I helped Mittie gather broom weed for Mrs. Roe to make brooms. Though we were out in the weeds, Mittie insisted on wearing her new dress and a matching hair ribbon. That girl is hopeless. Still no word from Mr. Roe, so Mittie and her mother will have to do all the broom making this year.

Later in the day, a courier brought word that our troops were near San Antonio. The little cannon had been so cantankerous, with its wheels smoking from the friction, they had to bury it in Sandy Creek not far from here. So much for their only piece of artillery. I wonder if Mrs. DeWitt's fine flag was buried, too.

★ ★ ★

Thursday, October 22

Lem returned from Dimitt's Landing. He said the ship had not arrived from the States and that all the farmers' cotton bales were lined up on the docks and along the river where farmers had waited in vain for barges to take the cotton downstream to the landing. American ships are afraid to come into Mexican waters during a war. We are greatly disappointed.

Papa told Lem he would have to kill a hog real soon. Lem's face turned all dark and cloudy and I saw him swallow hard. He loves critters so much, he doesn't even like killing snakes. Most everyone's pigs and hogs are left out running loose to root around the forest as they please. But pigs will come into the yard for food scraps.

When Papa saw Lem's face, he said, "You've got to learn to kill hogs sooner or later, son. Nobody likes killing hogs, but it's got to be done or else we starve over the winter." Poor Lem.

Friday, October 23

A big wind came up and gusted through the cracks in the logs all night, blowing right on my face. The window shutters rattled and the wind whistled around the corners and chimney so fierce that I tossed and turned all night.

Today, while Papa nailed the shutters over the windows, Green and I gathered buckets of river bottom clay and mud to fill the chinks. As usual, Green piddled around and didn't do one half the work I did, but took all the credit when Papa said we'd done a fine job. I didn't even argue.

Saturday, October 24

Last night Mama heated rocks in the fireplace and wrapped them in rags to keep our feet warm. We pulled down the winter quilts from the loft and patched the places where mice had nibbled on them. The wind whistled like a demon all night but didn't get through the cracks and I was proud that I had done a good job with the chinking.

I was awakened in the early morning by the most awful noise. The wind blew a tree against the chimney and knocked a chunk out of the flue. At sunrise, Mama told me and Green to fetch buckets of white-colored clay from the post oak grove. Then we gathered armfuls of dry sage grass that grows in tall clumps in the fields. We put the mud in a big tub then added the grass and some water and stomped it with our bare feet until it was mixed proper. My feet got cold as icicles. Papa's leg wouldn't allow him to climb up the ladder to the roof, so Lem did the chimney patching.

The finished job looked lopsided and lumpy. Papa grunted and shook his head and said Lem should have been more careful. Seems like Lem can't ever do anything right in Papa's eyes. But Mama told Lem it looked plumb good. She started a fire in the hearth right away to help speed up the curing of the clay. I fibbed and said the chimney looked as good as new. But Papa's words pierced Lem's heart and he tore off into the woods and didn't come home till dark.

Sunday, October 25

A miserable morning with heavy rains. Mittie came over after lunch. We gathered poke greens in the woods and took some to Susanna Dickinson. She thanked us and we watched over little Angelina again while Susanna cooked the poison out of the greens. Susanna told us she misses her husband desperately. When I whispered to Mittie, "Susanna is madly in love with Almeron," Mittie snorted and said, "Married folks are never madly in love." I said, "That's not so, Mittie Roe. My folks care for each other deeply and would hate to be separated." I saw the tears well up in Mittie's eyes and she ran out the door. It occurred to me she was thinking of her missing pa and I felt awful for my careless words. How I wish that man would come back or at least write and end Mittie's worries.

Monday, October 26

I spied a perfect clump of mistletoe up in a thorny mesquite tree. I will keep my eye on it for Christmas and hang it above the door. I have never been kissed by a boy nor a man, except for relatives, and they do not count. Mittie claims there is nothing to it, but she is not tongue-tied and goose-brained like me. Flirting and chatty conversation comes natural to her. As for kissing, I can think of nothing else on earth that I want and fear so much at the same time.

Tuesday, October 27

I walked to Mittie's house in hopes of getting a school lesson, but Mrs. Roe was too busy to teach. When I got there, she was chopping wood with an ax about as big and heavy as she is. With the town's men gone, it's that way with most of the families. I saw a woman killing a rabbit with a sling. She said her husband had taken their only gun, and the family had no meat.

Wednesday, October 28

Mama has been acting strange all day. She had one of her premonitions again. We have learned to respect her feelings, for she had a premonition before little Mary died, and before her own mother died of cholera. She fears something is going to happen to Willis and Uncle Henry.

Thursday, October 29

I saw a messenger riding to our house and my heart jumped to my throat. But it was good news. Our boys won their first battle, outside the old Concepción Mission south of San Antonio. Mama asked right away, "Was anybody hurt?" Papa had limped to the front porch and Mama was clinging to his arm. When the man said, "Nope. We didn't lose a man," Mama sighed. Papa patted her shoulder and said, "See there, you've been imagining things, Mrs. Lawrence."

The courier told us to spread the word that our boys need all the supplies we can spare. They're low on food and gunpowder and ammunition. The cold weather will set in soon and they have no blankets.

We spent the rest of the day scrounging for whatever we could spare. It wasn't much: one blanket, a bag of cornmeal, some onions and potatoes and dried beans, and a jar of honey. Lem hooked up the mules to the wagon and we kids climbed in. We took the supplies to the ferry and put them in one of the large cotton wagons that will take goods to the troops outside San Antonio. On a piece of paper, the man in charge noted what we had given and said the government of Texas would pay us later when the money was available. Papa laughed when we told him and said, "What government?"

Friday, October 30

Gathered pecans down by the river. Lem climbed the trees and shook down the ripe ones. The pecans along the Guadalupe River are the finest in Texas and fetch a grand price. Papa takes a wagon load to San Antonio every year for Uncle Isaac to sell in his store. But this year he will not go because of the war and because of

Volunteers and root hogs getting the nuts first. Picking pecans always reminds me that autumn has arrived and winter is not far behind.

Saturday, October 31

Tomorrow is Papa's birthday. We traded some of our pecans to Mr. Miller at the general store for a slab of chewing tobacco. Papa would rather smoke than chew, but times are hard. Mama says she has a surprise but would not tell us what it is.

Sunday, November 1

I heard Mama rustling around before dawn. When I woke up I smelled the most heavenly aroma on earth. I rushed to the table and saw a small pecan cake. Mama had traded sweet potatoes and pecans for some sugar and flour. Both are rare and expensive in the colonies.

Papa laughed when he saw the little cake. We divided it into five equal parts. Lem, Green, and Papa gobbled down their portions like starving pigs, but I divided mine into five perfect bites. Each one tasted better than the last and we all heaved a long sigh and licked the crumbs off our fingers. Papa said, "Thank you, Mrs. Lawrence. That was the tastiest cake I ever et." We gave Papa the tobacco. He said thank you and I swear there were tears in his eyes.

Monday, November 2

I am so mad I could dip snuff! Last night a goodly wind came up, so me, Green, and Lem got up early and hurried down to the river to gather fresh pecans. We spent the day filling our sacks and had a fine crop of big, delicious nuts. It was cold and our fingers ached, but we didn't mind, knowing the pecans would fetch a good deal in trade.

On the way back to the house we passed three scrubby-looking Volunteers. Each man had long, greasy hair, and whiskers on his unwashed face. They saw our bags and asked us what we had. Green blurted out that it was pecans. The three scoundrels claimed they shivered at night and starved half the time, and hadn't received any pay or stipend and the least they should get was a bag of pecans for fighting for Texas. I thought about poor Willis suffering and was so moved with guilt that I gave them my bag. Next thing I knew the two other men knocked my brothers to the ground and stole their bags of pecans. They shoved Lem's face in the mud.

Lem was furious, Green was crying, and I was shaking.

Lem ran off into the woods in humiliation, but Green told Mama as soon as we walked through the door. We did not tell Papa, as he would probably get all upset. I am sick about losing our pecans. I will never trust one of those Volunteers from the States again.

Tuesday, November 3

Half the hen eggs were missing yesterday, so this morning I got up very early to gather them. Three eggs were still wet and warm from just being laid. I saw two Volunteers creeping around the barn and ran inside and told Mama. She grabbed the old flintlock pistol and headed for the barn. She saw one of the men carrying a squawking hen by its feet. "Let go of that hen or it'll be the last thing you see," Mama shouted.

The man shrugged and cuddled the hen in his arms. "We're hungry, ma'am. We volunteered to help you Texians, but nobody gives us food or clothes or ammunition. How are we supposed to help if we're skin and bones?"

Mama lowered the barrel and sighed. She told him to come back later and she would give them cooked chicken. The man tipped his hat and let the chicken go. Mama picked out a pullet and wrung its neck. We plucked the feathers and Mama cooked a big pot of chicken for the man and made soup for us. The man returned at noon with two others and they ate every bit of chicken and cornbread as if it were their last meal on earth. Afterwards they sat with Papa on the front porch and talked for two hours. They came from the same part of Georgia where Papa was born. As they left, Papa gave them his birthday chewing tobacco.

Wednesday, November 4

The morning was warm, but by midday the temperature dropped as a blue norther rolled in. One half of the sky was a blue-black color and the other half was clear, as if the hand of God had painted a dividing line.

Papa, Lem, and Green dug a big hole in the yard and lowered a hog barrel down into it, tied with tackle and ropes attached to poles. The work was slow on account of Papa having to stop and rest his leg often. "Now all we need is a hog," Papa said.

I checked the hopper beside the house where we keep ashes from the hearth. I will need them to make lye water for the soap. Mama chopped extra wood and hauled it into the house. I pulled down the last quilt from the loft and put the cow and her calf into the barn. By nightfall sleet pelted the roof. We ate our supper by the fire, wrapped in every piece of clothing we had. Afterwards, Papa took out a curved knife and began sharpening it on a whetstone. After it was razor sharp, he said, "Lemuel, as soon as the storm lets up tomorrow, we'll kill that hog. Mrs. Lawrence will get her soap at last."

Lem muttered, "Yessir." He is miserable and I don't blame him. Hog killing is sad work.

Thursday, November 5

This morning I heard all kinds of grunting and snorting as Lem herded some hogs and sows into a little temporary pen and closed the gate. My heart ached as I watched Lem scratching the biggest hog behind the ears and talking to it.

"Time to get the water boiling," Mama said as Papa limped out the door, holding the sharpened knife. I was very thankful that Mama kept me and Green busy bringing buckets of water and sticks of firewood to the big iron cauldron in front of the cabin.

A hog's throat must be cut or stuck and the animal kept alive so it can bleed to death, or else the meat will be full of blood and spoil. The squealing is awful. Then they hoist the carcass up in the air and cut its belly open and the innards spill into a big tub. Mama will pick out the fat mixed with the entrails, then give the rest to the dogs. The work is disgusting and makes me sick, but it has to be done. Poor Lem. I saw him wipe his sleeve across his nose and knew he was crying.

The next chore was to lower the two-hundred-pound hog into the scalding barrel sunk in the ground and filled with boiling water. The water loosened the hog's hair and in a little while Papa and Lem moved the carcass to boards laid out on the ground. Papa scraped all the hair off the skin, then began butchering the hog into smaller portions. Mama took the tenderloin for making sausage.

As Papa carved out hams and shoulders and shanks, Lem packed them in a wooden barrel between layers of salt. While Mama cooked pieces of fat to render out the lard, Green fetched bundles of wood to keep the fire going. Mama poured the hot grease into crock jars to use for cooking and strained out the tiny brown bits of skin called "cracklings" to use for making soap. It took all day to kill and butcher the hog and the temperature didn't go above freezing. Our hands and feet were numb and we are still exhausted.

We ate fried hog liver and onions with cornbread

for supper. The menfolk are asleep now. Mama is still up. She is grinding the tenderloin with spices and herbs to make sausage. I offered to help, but she said for me to get a good night's sleep because tomorrow we will make soap.

Friday, November 6

Another cold, cold day, but I didn't mind because making soap is hot business. After breakfast, I fetched buckets of water and poured them over the ashes in the hopper at the side of the house to make lye water. Lem and Papa chopped more wood and got a fire going under the iron cauldron. Mama put in the lye water with the cracklings and we began our vigil. Hour after hour Mama and I took turns stirring the mixture with a big wooden battling stick. When the soap began to thicken and the cracklings gradually disappeared, I asked Mama if I might toss in some crushed berries to make the soap a purple color. But Mama said, "Brown soap was good enough for my mother; it's good enough for us."

When the mixture was thick, Mama doused the fire, and let it cool. By the end of the day when Mama broke it into pieces, we had our usual ugly brown soap. Mama is in high spirits. We have soap and pork, two things that make life bearable. If only Willis would come home, it would be a wonderful world.

Saturday, November 7

Papa hung the meat in the smokehouse and Green fanned a low fire all day to cure the hams. Mama sent me to Mrs. Roe's house carrying a large hunk of lye soap and a big slab of pork wrapped in cloth. Mittie was thrilled to see me, as cold weather and chores have kept us apart for days. School lessons are rare now. Were it not for my precious diary, I think I would forget how to write.

Later, Mittie and I were supposed to be multiplying our thirteens, but we were sneaking looks at fashion sketches in an old *Lady's Book* magazine, when we heard screams from down the street. We saw women and children running and strange men breaking down doors.

My heart started pounding and I said I'd better go home, but Mrs. Roe said, "No, Lucinda. It's not safe out there. Those men are on the rampage." She took down an old musket that looked as if it had not been fired since 1776. Mrs. Roe quickly tapped gunpowder from a horn into the barrel, then rammed in a piece of cotton wadding and dropped in the bullet and a little more wadding. Then she carefully poured a little more gunpowder into the flintlock chamber.

"Mama!" Mittie cried. "Are you going to shoot somebody?"

"If I have to. No scoundrel is going to harm my family. Take the butcher knife and hide the children under the bed. Kill anything that tries to get you."

We scrambled under the bed and shook like scared puppies. The sound of shouting men and breaking glass and splintering wood grew louder as the rampaging Volunteers got closer. Men's voices and heavy footsteps reached the front porch. Then I heard the thump of an ax against the door. Mittie began shaking and whimpering, so I put my hand over her mouth. The door crashed and Mrs. Roe said in a voice as hard as flint, "One step closer, sir, and I'll shoot." I peeked out and saw a scraggly man dressed in buckskin stopped in his tracks. He backed onto the dogtrot slowly. His friends laughed, and I saw that one of them was holding a bottle of corn liquor.

"We want our due," he said.

"Take another step and you'll receive your just due in Hades," Mrs. Roe said in an unwavering voice. The men shrugged and started to walk away. Mrs. Roe lowered the gun, and suddenly a third man came in the side window and grabbed her from behind. The musket went off, blowing a hole in the roof. Mrs. Roe screamed and before I knew what was happening, I jumped up and grabbed the skillet. I hit that awful man. He yelled and ran out, but not before his head had a bleeding gash in it.

Mittie and I bawled and hugged Mrs. Roe. I ran all the way home and met Mama on the path. She was walking faster than I'd ever seen her move before. When she saw me she shouted and hugged me so hard I couldn't breathe. A minute later Papa limped up and hugged me, too.

"We thought you'd been kilt for sure," Green chirped.

Later —

The whole Roe family came over. Mrs. Roe said the rampaging men were passing through on their way to San Antonio. They broke into every house in Gonzales, stealing food and possessions and molesting the women. The Roes are staying the night with us. It is crowded, but we feel more secure with so many of us.

Mittie is still shaking. She says I am the bravest girl in Texas and she vows she would be dead if I had not hit that man.

Sunday, November 8

The Roes stayed all day. Mama refused to let me go out alone. I helped Papa melt a piece of lead pipe and make more bullets. They were not very round, but he said I did a good job. We watched for the scoundrels all day, but they did not return.

Monday, November 9

Cold and rainy. We stayed in all day. Green is driving me insane. He makes faces and sticks things in his nose like an idiot. How I wish the weather would let up so he could go out.

Tuesday, November 10

After breakfast, Papa and Lem drove the Roes back to their house in the wagon. Mama and I were on needles and pins waiting for our men to get back. Mama wanted to wash clothes with the new lye soap, but

Papa advised her to stay inside behind barricaded doors while he was gone.

Papa and Lem were gone a very long time. When they returned Papa was in a tolerable good mood — the Convention in San Felipe has not declared Texas's independence after all. They signed a document declaring that Texas will remain loyal to Mexico, but Texians will fight to restore the old Mexican Constitution of 1824, the one that Santa Anna abolished.

Wednesday, November 11

We received a letter from Willis in San Antonio. It says:

Dearest Mother, Father, brothers, and little sister:

There have been no more fights with the Mexicans. Everyone is hungry and cold. We are on the constant prowl for food. When we left we were still wearing only our thin summer clothes, thinking the war would be over in a week's time. But if the cold doesn't kill us, then surely the boredom will. The enemy seems content to stay inside town and there is nothing to do all day except throw knives and have shooting contests. General Austin told us to save our ammunition, so even that is forbidden. Volunteers from New Orleans arrived and boasted of being the best shots in the States, so naturally some of our Texian boys had to prove them otherwise. Many local Mexicans — they call themselves Tejanos for they come from Texas — have joined our forces. They despise Santa Anna, too.

I would be obliged if you could send me a warmer shirt and all the gunpowder and lead you can find. Some are tired of this waiting and say they will return home if they don't get to fight soon. I know as soon as General Austin decides to attack San Antonio, the victory will be ours. We are eager and ready to fight, if the enemy would but show his face. Do not worry about me. My love to all of you,

Willis James Lawrence

I cannot finish my diary entry. My heart is aching too much for dear Willis. I keep imagining him in his thin blue cotton shirt and only one quilt to cover him from the cold.

Sunday, November 15

Oh, my precious, precious diary! You were lost but now you are found. For three days I searched in vain and cried my eyes out. And all because of Green and his mischievous ways. Being in a pure ornery mood, he grabbed my diary while I sat on the front porch Wednesday evening after supper. He and Lemuel tossed it back and forth out of my reach. I screamed until I was blue in the face but to no avail. Then Green threw my diary up on the roof. Papa made Lemuel climb up to fetch it, but when he got there my diary had vanished. I climbed up myself, tearing the hem on my dress, and looked over every inch of the cedar shakes. I suspected Green and Lem were in cahoots, and called them every kind of thief and liar. On the second day Papa got tired of our bickering and laid into Lem and Green with a hickory switch. Even then, they did not confess and swore they did not take my diary.

This morning Lemuel ran up and interrupted our Sunday Bible reading. He said he had a miracle to show me. All of us, even Papa, walked to the woods at the edge of the clearing and watched Lemuel climb up a tall tree and reach inside a big hollow. He pulled out my diary and dropped it down. Little pointed teeth marks covered the leather and some of the pages had been chewed on.

"B–Bandit d–decided to have a r–reading l–lesson," Lem said. That ol' coon seemed to know his name for he climbed down the tree and crawled all over Lem's shoulders. He stuck his little thieving paws into Lem's pocket and fished out a piece of beef jerky. We all laughed so hard we shed tears. I told Green and Lem I was sorry for accusing them, but it was still their faults for causing all the trouble.

Monday, November 16

Green is still mad at me for the unjust thrashing he got. At bedtime he announced that he was going to sleep with Lemuel from now on, as he was tired of being surrounded by cruel women. Mama said, "Oh, my little man is growing up," and helped him move his pallet and pillow to the room across the dogtrot. Since Willis is away, there is space but it is much colder than the main room where Mama does all the cooking. I pretended good riddance, but it feels strangely empty now, without Green's excited whispers as he tells me his secrets, and the sounds of his little snoring squeaks.

Wednesday, November 18

Today is Mittie's fifteenth birthday. Mrs. Roe is allowing her to spend the night with me. Mittie taught me the custom of the salty egg. All the excitement and giggling reminded me of the good times we used to have. Before bedtime, we boiled up two eggs, cut them in halves, scooped out the yolks, and filled the cavities with salt. We ate those salty eggs, giggling and gagging. No matter how thirsty we get tonight, we cannot drink. While we sleep we will dream that a boy brings us a dipper of fresh water. And whoever that boy is will be our future husband. Mittie knows I want to dream of Galba, but she still refuses to tell me who she fancies. Oh, my throat longs for water. I do not think I can bear it another minute. Water! Water! I need water!

Thursday, November 19

Upon waking, I drank a dipper full of water without pausing. So did Mittie. I am so happy. I did dream that Galba brought me a drink. I saw his face as clear as day. Mittie wouldn't tell me who she dreamed about until I tackled her to the floor and got her hands behind her back. Green tickled her ribs until she had tears in her eyes. Finally, she shouted out, "It was Lem. Can you believe it? Plain as a post, Lemuel Lawrence. I told you I'll never marry a dirt farmer." I started laughing so hard my side hurt. Mittie got spitting mad. She grabbed her bonnet and left. Mama says I was rude to laugh so much since the Roes are going through a hard time. I will apologize to Mittie the next time I see her. Still — I cannot stop laughing when I think about her in a fancy dress and Lem in his dirty buckskin, and Bandit as a groomsman at the wedding.

Saturday, November 21

Mama is sewing a winter shirt for Willis. She dragged the big trunk down from the storage loft and took out her one and only fancy dress, made of thick, warm, blue velvet. Her calloused hands looked out of place stroking that smooth, soft velvet. She didn't say anything, but I know it pained her to cut it into pieces. I cut the scraps into useful shapes and neatly stacked them in the big basket where Mama keeps her quilt makings.

Papa decided to take supplies and Willis's new shirt to San Antonio. I helped Mama bake extra cornbread and pack food. Papa and Lem hitched the mule to the wagon and left at daybreak this morning. They took the old pistol, all the gunpowder, and some handmade bullets. I used honey to make some sweet johnnycakes for them. The velvet shirt turned out very nice. Green sent Willis his good blanket. That was so sweet of the little monkey. Papa told us not to worry, but as he hugged me good-bye I felt strangely sad.

Sunday, November 22

Rained all day. The hills are ablaze with red, yellow, orange, and brown all mixed in with the green of the cedar trees. The beauty takes my breath away.

Mama misses Papa so much. She didn't even want me to comb her hair. I did anyway. It feels uncommonly quiet with no men in the house — no boots on the doorstep, no pipe smoke in the room, no arguing and laughing. Mama let me and Green sleep in the big bed with her, one of us on each side, the cat all cozy on top of our feet.

Monday, November 23

Too much rain and wind to wash clothes. Mama started a new quilt. She let me choose the color for the border around each square. I picked the blue velvet. We have some red and yellow calico scraps, a bit of green, and the rest is mostly brown, white, and dull gray. There is one nice piece of rosy pink. Mama says she will think of something special for that. She also cut some strips for a new bonnet for me, as my old one is filthy and ragged.

Tuesday, November 24

Bright and sunny, but cold. Mama said, with the men away, there wasn't much need to wash and iron. I walked to Mittie's, trying not to step in mud puddles. I saw Susanna Dickinson outside with her little girl. Baby Angelina looks prettier every time I see her, with her black curly hair now hanging to her shoulders. Susanna asked me and Mittie if we would watch her while she ground corn in her steel mill. Angelina is terrified of the loud racket, so we took her to the general store and let her play with the pots and pans.

Later, I asked Susanna if she had heard from her husband. She sighed loud enough to rattle the trees and said, "He sent a message that he is fine and misses us." Her chin quivered as she spoke. "If he misses us so much, why didn't he take us with him? If Almeron comes back alive, I swear I will never leave his side again. I'd rather die alongside him in the heat of battle than at the hands of those awful scoundrels who broke into our house." She wiped her tears then picked up Angelina and went inside. I could hear her crying through the window.

Poor Susanna doesn't seem like herself anymore. Nobody does. This war is fraying all of our nerves. I wish it had never started.

Wednesday, November 25

Rainy. More piecing of quilt squares. Mama has finished ten squares and I have done four. A neighbor came over and helped Mama. They talked for hours and Mama didn't cook dinner. Green and I had warmed-over red beans and cornbread. He grumbled but I said Mama needs a day off from cooking.

Thursday, November 26

Thank goodness the rain stopped and Green has gone out to explore. Mama asked me to comb some cotton to make batting for the quilt. We keep the extra cotton up in the attic. I dreaded it and sure enough a big black widow spider fell right on my face. I screamed so loud Mama dropped her quilt square and leaped to her feet. She was halfway to the fire poker before she realized it wasn't an Indian attack. She held her hand over her heaving bosom and laughed, the first laughing I've seen her do in days. I spent the day combing and cording cotton for the spinning wheel.

Friday, November 27

Cotton, cotton, I am so sick of cotton. My hands ache from combing the fibers back and forth until they are soft, then rolling them into long cords. Mama finished up the last square for the quilt and sewed them together. Since our quilting frame is broken, we will go to Mrs. Roe's house tomorrow to use hers. Mama cooked a delicious stew to take.

Saturday, November 28

The Roe house was full of life today. Mama, me, Mittie, Susanna, and three other women, and a dozen younguns were there. After Mrs. Roe pulled the quilt frame down from the ceiling, they stretched a sheet of plain white muslin over the frame, laid out the cotton batting, then covered it with the quilt top. The women cackled like happy hens as they sewed the top to the bottom, using tiny stitches shaped into lovely curves. Mama saved the piece of pink cloth for the center square and made it look like a rose, with green petals. It is beautiful.

★ ★ ★

Monday, November 30

Hallelujah! Papa and Lem came back today. They had so much news that they sat on top of the wagon in the middle of town and answered questions for nearly a full hour. Lem had a knapsack full of letters scribbled from the men camped outside San Antonio and he handed them out to the wives with great dignity and ceremony. There had been a little grass fight and another Texian victory. Stephen F. Austin had been appointed commissioner to the United States and left for the purpose of raising funds and more Volunteers for the Texas army. Col. Burleson is now in charge of the Texians at San Antonio.

Papa is exhausted. The long wagon trip aggravated his leg wound, and he is suffering something fierce. He grimaced when he lowered himself onto Mama's new quilt. He didn't even notice it, but I whispered in his ear, "Do you like Mama's new quilt?" and he winked at me and said, "Why, Mrs. Lawrence, I do believe this is the best quilt you've ever made. That blue velvet border looks right nice." Mama said, "Oh, it's not my best at all, Mr. Lawrence, the pieces are plumb crooked." But I saw her smile when she thought we weren't looking.

Mama cooked the best supper we've had in ages to celebrate Papa's return, but Papa fell asleep before it was ready. Mama said not to wake him.

Tuesday, December 1

When Papa awakened this morning, he told us he had received a bit of news about Uncle Isaac, who is one of the few Anglos who live in Spanish-speaking San Antonio. He is fine but Aunt Esperanza is bedridden, very ill because of being with child. All other Anglos have left town, but Uncle Isaac refuses to leave his wife.

Mama's face clouded at the news. She twisted her apron until it looked like a rope. Then she excused herself and said she had to go dig some potatoes for supper. I saw her behind the smokehouse sitting beside Baby Mary's grave marker. I know she is wrestling with decisions.

Wednesday, December 2

We received a note from Uncle Henry down in Goliad. He says he is fine except for a little cough. The presidio where the Texians are staying is dark and

dank. Uncle Henry also sent a letter addressed to Aunt
Nancy in San Felipe. Mama asked me to write a line at
the bottom of Aunt Nancy's letter. It says, "I hope this
war is over before the end of February when Esperanza's baby is due. I plan to go to San Antonio come
what may."

Thursday, December 3

Some men returned from San Antonio. They said
the whole army is falling apart. Morale is so low nearly
every Texian talks about leaving so he can be home
with his family for Christmas. I wish Willis would
come back, but Papa said he is strong-willed and probably having the adventure of his life. I cannot imagine
having a Christmas without him to shoot a turkey.

Friday, December 4

Papa's leg wound has opened and festered again and
his fever has returned. The doctor lanced the wound
and gave Papa whiskey for the pain. Blood got on
Mama's new quilt, but she didn't complain.

★ ★ ★

Saturday, December 5

Papa was in a state of confusion all day, not knowing what was going on around him. Lem and Mama had to tie him to the bed to keep him from getting up and walking on his hurt leg. I am so fearful of gangrene. If it spreads, the doctor will have to amputate.

Sunday, December 6

Late this evening an express courier passed through on his way to San Felipe with urgent news. The Texians finally attacked San Antonio and a battle is now raging. The word spread like wildfire and within minutes a crowd gathered around the messenger. He said an old soldier named Ben Milam got tired of waiting and figured now was the best time for battle, no matter what Col. Burleson said. The soldier drew a line in the sand with his sword and called out, "Boys, who will follow old Ben Milam into San Antonio?" Of the five hundred men camped there, three hundred said, "I will, I will" and stepped over the line.

Green asked me, "Cinda, if the Texians are attacking San Antonio, how will they know not to shoot at Uncle Isaac's house?" I couldn't bear to see that sorrowful look on my little brother's face, so I told him Uncle Isaac would put a secret sign on his front door so that the Texians wouldn't attack it. A wave of relief flooded his dirty face. How I wish that I believed my own words. I cannot help but think of Willis in the heat of battle. I wonder what he is feeling, how scared he is. And what if he shoots Uncle Isaac by mistake? I hate my head for harboring such thoughts, but they will not leave me alone.

Monday, December 7

Mama got up before dawn and started working like a whirlwind and did chores all day. She said as long as she keeps busy she won't think about Willis, Uncle Isaac, and Aunt Esperanza. I started to mention Uncle Henry in Goliad and Aunt Nancy in San Felipe with five children, but decided to leave well enough alone.

Papa's fever broke this evening. He will not lose his leg. Thank you, Lord.

Tuesday, December 8

I helped Mittie trim broom weed and cut twigs off hickory limbs for broom handles. Christmas is a busy time for them, as many women order new brooms or receive them as gifts. No one mentions Mr. Roe anymore, and most are starting to treat Mittie's mother like a widow.

Green and some local boys have been drawing lines in the dirt with sticks, and shouting, "Who will stand and fight ol' Santy Anny?" They spout simple challenges like, "Who will follow me to the general store?" or "Who will go with me to the cotton gin?" All the little boys cross the lines with great ceremony. Today an older boy, annoyed with the young ones in the street, scratched a line with his chopping hoe and yelled, "Who will go with me into the rattlesnake den on Miller's farm?" He was only joshing, but the boys got scared looks on their faces. Only Green and one other boy stepped over the line, their little faces all serious and dignified. It made me think of Willis. I believe that if the time ever comes, he will be one of the first to step over the line, no matter what the danger.

Wednesday, December 9

Another express messenger passed through town. He said the battle in San Antonio was still raging when he left. The Texians and their Tejano allies were going from house to house fighting the Mexicans hand to hand. General Cos, the Mexican leader, who just happens to be Santa Anna's own brother-in-law, is now holed up in the old mission called the Alamo, cut off from his supplies.

Thursday, December 10

Gonzales is very quiet today. Nearly every house has a man fighting in San Antonio, whether it be a husband, a father, a brother, a son, or an uncle. I could almost hear the prayers going up to Heaven tonight.

Friday, December 11

Praise the Lord! Our boys have declared victory! General Cos surrendered and San Antonio is ours. Most wondrous of all, only four Texians were killed, though we were sad to learn that Mr. Ben Milam, who led the charge, was one of them. Mama was so happy to hear that Willis and Uncle Isaac were spared, that she broke out into singing "Amazing Grace." This evening at bedtime, she took my hand and led a prayer for the dead and wounded, including the Mexicans. When I asked her why she grieved for the Mexicans, too, she said, "It's a sin to take pleasure in the death of any human, be he friend or foe." I wonder if she would say the same if Willis had been killed.

Later —

More news from San Antonio. General Cos not only surrendered the Alamo mission, but he gave up all the weapons inside it, which is rumored to be about twenty cannons, some rifles, and gunpowder. But best of all, General Cos agreed that he would withdraw all troops from Texas. There are those who say Col. Burleson made a big mistake not executing the Mexicans because they are not to be trusted, but Papa said it is not honorable to kill soldiers whose general has surrendered. I heard one man shout, "Santa Anna will retaliate with vengeance when he finds out about his brother-in-law's humiliating defeat." But a lot of folks feel the war is over. Now our men can return and we can get on with our lives. I miss my school lessons dearly.

Saturday, December 12

The Texians are returning home in droves, stopping over in Gonzales before heading back to the other settlements. They are full of stories of shooting and

Mexican bayonets and blood. Lem doesn't like such talk, but Green listens with his mouth open wide enough to trap horseflies. Rumor has it that all of our men will be home for Christmas. Out of the original five hundred men camped outside San Antonio, only one hundred and fifty have stayed, mostly those rowdy Volunteers from the States. They say the streets of San Antonio are filled with celebrations.

Sunday, December 13

No time for Bible reading this morning. A steady stream of men is passing through on the way back to the colonies. Every time I turn around there is some new man at the door. Mama says she will not cook on the Sabbath, but she will turn no man away who needs food. So far there is no sign of Willis.

Monday, December 14

When is that Willis coming home? We know he is well, because every man we ask says he was whooping in the streets of San Antonio with the others. Oh, another man is knocking at the door. Claims to be Papa's distant cousin from Georgia. Seems half the Texas army consists of Papa's cousins from Georgia.

85

Tuesday, December 15

Mama is losing patience. She says if Willis does not come home soon, she will go and fetch him back by the ears.

Wednesday, December 16

At last my dear brother has come home. Mama scolded him for being so tardy, then hugged him till he nearly turned blue. We piled all over him, and even Papa crawled out of bed and limped over to give his son a hug.

Willis spent the whole day sitting in front of the fire telling tales of the battles he took part in. I kept the fire going and Mama worked at her spinning wheel. "We fought house to house," he said, standing up and waving his arms. "Soon as we'd take one house, the Mexicans would fall back to another one. I was penned in, thinking all was over, when I heard a shout from a house and then saw a Mexican flag with the numbers 1824 painted across it waving in the window. I figured it was a friendly Tejano, so I ducked into that house. It was Uncle Isaac's house!"

Mama gasped and stopped her spinning. "Is he all right?" she asked.

"Sure is. After the battle, I stayed with him for three days." When Willis said Aunt Esperanza is feeling poorly, Mama frowned and said, "I pray all the excitement doesn't affect her birthing time."

Later, Mrs. Roe brought Willis a cake. Mittie gave him a bouquet of wild daisies, the last ones of the season. Her face turned rosy when he placed a soft little thank-you kiss on her cheek. Willis ended his tales by saying, "We don't have to worry about Santa Anna. Now he knows we're not willing to sit back and let him take our freedom. It'll be a long time before he tries anything again."

Papa smoked his pipe, and though his brows twisted, he didn't say anything. I think he didn't want to spoil Willis's moment of glory. When it got dark, Willis escorted the Roes back to their house. He got back very late. I was the only one up, writing in my diary by dim candlelight. He hugged me hard and said he had missed us more than words could say. He is snoring like thunder in the mountains now, but I don't mind at all.

Thursday, December 17

The call has come out for more supplies for the Volunteers still in Texas. Though some believe the war is over, others think that Santa Anna and his brother-in-law will be back with an even bigger army. In town I heard citizens complaining about having to give so much food and supplies to the Volunteers. Of all the settlements in Texas, Gonzales has done the most, because we are the closest to San Antonio.

But we have no more to give. Our corn is gone except for the seed corn; we have no more blankets or quilts or cloth. Mama measured out all the coffee except for a handful and put it in a bag. Then she cut off three big hunks of the lye soap. Papa said to give them the last of the beef jerky left over from the slaughtered ox and some of the ham. Green began complaining about having to smoke another hog, but Willis shamed him by saying, "Those men in San Antonio are willing to give their lives for freedom. Don't you think the least we can do is give them a few pieces of pork?"

Friday, December 18

Papa and Willis killed and butchered a hog early this morning. Lemuel ducked out of sight early and was gone all day. But he brought in a slab of honeycomb dripping with luscious honey, so he was forgiven. He also brought in a black crow that had a broken wing. He bandaged the wing up nicely and built a little cage out of dry reeds from the river. He fed the crow corn and the bird seemed right pleased and plumb friendly. Lem said he was going to teach it to talk and fetch things for him. Mama said we didn't need another critter to feed. Willis said the Indians believe a crow is a bad omen. I hope not.

Saturday, December 19

Willis was right about the bad omen. A band of Comanche raided nearby farms yesterday. They are a most bothersome lot, stealing horses and cattle. The Kechi and Wacos and Tonkawas rarely cause trouble. A few years back, Mama befriended an old Tonkawa. He had white hair and was half blind. He traded Mama all kinds of handmade items for cornmeal and cornbread. He gave me a doll made of clay and horsehair. He died of old age.

Sunday, December 20

Went to Mittie's house. We conspired all day what to give our families for Christmas. Wasn't much we could do — no cloth for clothes, no yarn for knitting, no thread for sewing, no flour nor sugar for sweets. We gathered up corn shucks and some tiny scraps of calico and made dolls for her little sisters. We will meet again tomorrow with more plans.

Monday, December 21

Met Mittie. We walked to the woods and got a bucket of the white clay from under the oak trees. We shaped big marbles for her little brother and for Green and baked them in hot coals in Mittie's backyard so they would harden. While we were in the woods I spied a soft spot in the ground and dug up a bag of fresh pecans. It looked just like the one the rowdy Volunteer had stolen from Lem back in November. Whoever hid it must have forgotten it was there.

Mrs. Roe said I could have a tiny bit of whiskey to soak the pecans in if I would give her some, too. I cracked and shelled the pecans and while they were soaking in whiskey, I wove a little basket out of straw to put them in. When I said, "Papa will love these," Mittie got all sulky. I forgot I am not supposed to mention the word *papa*.

★ ★ ★

Tuesday, December 22

Had an idea this morning. After chores, I grabbed Green and hastened to an old abandoned cabin on the other side of the woods. It was a good two miles or more, but I figured I might find a few pieces of colored glass in the yard. With an abandoned place, you never know what you might come across. The old place was falling down. The chimney had caved in and the roof had burnt, probably from a lightning strike. We scrounged all over the place and here is what I found: one horseshoe, three bent horseshoe nails, a pocketful of watermelon seeds, and another pocketful of hollyhock seeds. Here is what Green found: a broken pitchfork tine, a cow's horn, an arrowhead, and some strips of cowhide. I made him throw away the cowhide strips as they were mostly rotted. It isn't much but it will have to do.

Wednesday, December 23

Most all the Gonzales men are back home from San Antonio. I saw Almeron Dickinson playing with his little daughter, Angelina. He was telling Susanna he was worried about the boys left behind in San

Antonio. If Santa Anna decides to attack, there will be no one to defend the Alamo. When Almeron said he planned to return there soon, Susanna's blue eyes blazed with fire. She leaned down and whispered to me, "I'm not staying behind this time, no matter what he says." I suspect Susanna will get her way.

Many of the Volunteers from the States are still camped outside our town. I saw one of them standing in front of the general store. He was looking so forlorn I asked Mr. Miller what was wrong.

"That man wanted to buy some paper to write a letter home, but there's not a sheet of paper to be found in these parts." My heart ached for the poor fellow, so I tugged his sleeve and told him he could have a sheet of my diary. I never saw a face light up so much. He thanked me profusely and said he would pay me back as soon as he could.

I plucked the clump of mistletoe from the mesquite tree today. Why I bother, I do not know. Who would want to kiss a long-legged goose like me?

Thursday, December 24

I am almost too exhausted to write. The menfolk are asleep and their snores fill the cabin. Mama is still plucking feathers from the plump turkey that Willis brought in late this afternoon. He left at dawn with Galba. Galba yanked my pigtail and called me "Petunia." I stuck out my tongue and called him "Pumpkin Face." Oh, why do I always do such childish things when I am around him? No wonder he thinks of me as a little girl. Though I'm three years younger than he, I'm tall for my age and could pass for fourteen if I could keep my mouth from making stupid blunders every time he is around. I did not have the nerve to hang the mistletoe above the door, for fear he would see it and run away.

I got up at dawn and cleaned the house from top to bottom, taking out all the furniture, then scrubbing the puncheon floors, then sweeping all the dust and cobwebs from every nook and corner. I beat the dust out of the little braided rag rugs and the buffalo skin rug that Lemuel sleeps on. Dug sweet potatoes and onions from the garden and picked the last of the peas and shucked a dozen ears of dried corn. Papa helped me select a big pumpkin and sharpened a gourd so I could scoop out the insides and seeds. I cooked the pumpkin meat in boiling water, then mashed it up real good, and watched Mama make pumpkin pie with freshly gathered eggs, sugar, and cream. Then she let me roll out the piecrust with a rolling pin. Christmas is the only time of the year we have pie, as sugar and flour are so scarce. Sometimes we use honey instead of sugar, or molasses, but this year Mama said she is not going to skimp on anything. And I know why. Pumpkin is Willis's favorite.

Green and Lemuel gathered boughs of fresh cedar from the hills to put over the mantel and on the doors. The house smells so fresh and delicious. Just this minute I offered to help pluck the turkey, but Mama said the job's almost done. She hugged me and kissed my forehead and said thank you for cleaning the house and making it look so good. Mama looks tired. I wish I had something special to give her, but I know no matter what useless trinket she receives from each of us, she will smile and say it is just what she needed.

Friday, December 25

I awakened before the sun was up and saw that Mama was still by the hearth. I think she stayed up all night. The turkey was roasting on a spit over a low fire. It must have been the wonderful smell that woke me up. I hugged Mama's waist and said Merry Christmas. She reached into her apron pocket and gave me a little gift wrapped in a scrap of blue velvet and told me to go ahead and open it before the menfolk got up. It was a beautiful ivory button, carved to look like a rose. It came from her mother's wedding gown and I knew that it was precious to her and worth much because over the years in emergencies, Mama had sold all the other buttons like it. I threw my arms around Mama's neck and kissed her face, still warm from the heat of the fire. It didn't matter what else I got; this was the most precious gift I could receive.

I gave Mama her gift, embarrassed that it was so pitiful. It was the hollyhock seeds wrapped in a scrap of red calico. Mama's eyes lit up. "Why, Lucinda, how did you know that hollyhocks are my most favorite flower in the world? I can hardly wait for spring. My garden will be the envy of all Gonzales." Then she kissed me and squeezed my hand. About that time Green woke up and there was no peace and quiet again all day.

It was the most wonderful Christmas I've ever enjoyed. Everyone was so happy. Green liked his marbles and set to playing with them right away. I gave Lem the arrowhead and I gave Papa and Willis the whiskey pecans. Willis told us he had a big surprise, but would wait until the Roe family arrived to show us. Papa made Mama a new wood spindle for her spinning wheel.

When the Roes arrived, they were all smiles and

carrying a big Mexican straw basket. That sly Willis had bought all of us presents in San Antonio and then asked Mrs. Roe to keep them hidden until today. What a surprise! He gave Mama sticks of cinnamon bark and Papa a passel of hot peppers. He gave me a big chunky Spanish candle. Mrs. Roe gave Mama a fine new broom, like she does every year. Mittie was wearing her new dress and a pretty red hair ribbon. She said Willis gave it to her. I am eaten alive with jealousy. Why didn't he give me a hair ribbon, too?

We feasted today until my stomach ached. After lunch, Mittie flaunted her new hair ribbon in my face. I showed her my Spanish candle and the ivory button and said they suited me fine and were more useful than a hair ribbon. Mittie said they were nice, but a hair ribbon was what every girl wanted for Christmas. She is my best friend, but I was glad when she left.

In the afternoon, Mama, Green, and I loaded the basket with food and took it to the men camped outside town. They looked mighty sad, being away from home on Christmas day. Mama said, "I wonder if you fellows would like some Christmas turkey. We have more than we need." The men took their hats off and thanked her like little kids getting toys. Green offered them one of his marbles, and though they didn't take it, I never felt more proud of the little imp. As we were leaving, the man who I had given the paper from my diary to walked up and handed me a pretty blue ribbon. My eyes nearly popped out. He said it was in thanks for my kindness. Mama smiled all the way home and said I had learned a lesson in life, that unselfish kindness is always rewarded in one way or another.

Saturday, December 26

I heard a fiddle and harmonica playing all night in the camps. I couldn't help but feel sorry for the Volunteers. Why are they still here? If the war is over, shouldn't they go back to the States?

Sunday, December 27

Nobody is working because it's the Sabbath and because it's still Christmas holidays. Haven't seen Mittie in two days and that suits me fine. The little blue ribbon I got is too small for my hair so I am using it as a marker in my diary. Maybe I won't even tell Mittie about it.

★ ★ ★

Monday, December 28

Willis and I fought over the turkey wishbone and pulled it apart. He got the short end. I stuck out my tongue and taunted him, saying he will die first. He got a funny look on his face and I felt awful.

Tuesday, December 29

A man rode by, carrying letters from the States. We received a short letter from Mama's cousin in Nachitoches, Louisiana. It was dated October 1:

Dearest Rebecca — I am sorry to bear sad news. There is a smallpox epidemic here in Nachitoches. So many have died. My husband and two babies have passed on. One of the citizens from Gonzales was here and died. I believe he was the husband of our second cousin, Sarah — a Mr. Thomas Roe.

I couldn't bear to read any more and put the letter down.

"Oh, Mama — Mr. Roe didn't run off after all," I cried. "All those horrible things people said about him deserting his family and all the pain Mittie and Mrs.

Roe had to bear. It isn't fair." My eyes teared up and I ran into Mama's arms. Papa patted Mama's shoulder and said, "Thomas was a right nice gentleman. Do you want me to give the news to Sarah?"

Mama shook her head and drew in a deep breath. "No, Mr. Lawrence. I think it will be easier on her coming from my lips." I dreaded facing Mittie with the word, but knew I needed to go, too. When we arrived, Mrs. Roe and Mama had a long cry in each other's arms, and so did me and Mittie. Poor, poor Mittie. Her heart is breaking in two. I feel awful inside, knowing I acted so childish and was unkind to her when I should have been a better friend. I swear here and now to never, never be jealous of her red hair ribbons or her dresses again.

Thursday, December 31

The family gathered around the fire and I read the latest news from the *Telegraph and Texas Register* that arrived today. The biggest news is that David Crockett is on his way to Texas from Tennessee with some followers. Lem, Willis, and Green whooped, "Davy Crockett!" at the same time when they heard that. There is hardly a more famous man and we are all hoping he stops in Gonzales on his way to San Antonio.

Friday, January 1, 1836

A new year is here. I pray it will be better than the wretched one that has just passed. I wish things would return to normal — I miss my school lessons and the old Mittie who used to be so much fun. My New Year's resolutions are these: be kinder to Mittie, be more patient with Lem and Green, help Mama and Papa more, learn the multiplication tables all the way through.

Lem's raccoon, Bandit, got into the corncrib and Papa said he was going to shoot that varmint, so Lem took Bandit five miles away and left him in a tree hollow with a pouch of corn and a catfish he'd caught in the river. Poor Lem, he looked miserable when he got back. If it weren't for his pet crow, I suppose his heart would be broken.

Saturday, January 2

The holidays are officially over. Papa and the boys got to work splitting rails for a new fence and clearing out brush and saplings. Even Green had to work in the fields removing rocks. We have forgotten what farming is like, with the holidays and the war distracting us so long. Mama asked me to tear a sheet from my diary and write a letter to Uncle Isaac in San Antonio. It says:

Dearest Brother Isaac,

I hope and pray that Esperanza is doing well and that her baby will not come too early. I urge her to stay in bed. I have told Mr. Lawrence that I am going to San Antonio, come what may, to help with the birthing of this child. I plan to leave in early February. Send word if there is any change in Esperanza's health.

Your devoted sister, Rebecca

Papa is dead set against Mama going, for he says it is still dangerous there. They are now engaged in a battle of wills, though they do not shout.

Sunday, January 3

Walked to Mittie's house, but she feels too poorly to talk. Every conversation on the street I overheard says there will be more war this spring.

Tuesday, January 5

I heard a noise at my window at daybreak and looked out a crack in the shutters. I saw a gray face with a black mask — Bandit is back!

Lem was so happy to see the furry critter he cried.

Papa got a case of softheartedness and told Lem he could keep the raccoon as long as it stayed out of the corncrib. Lem spent all day building a raccoon-proof crib. All the while Lem worked, that crazy coon climbed over his back and played with his hat. Then the crow landed on his shoulder. Lem looked like a forest king. He swears the crow can talk. It's supposed to be saying, "Let's go fishing," but it sounds like gibberish to me.

Wednesday, January 6

Two neighbors came over and sat on the front porch with Papa and Willis. They whittled sticks and talked about war and politics. One man said he was moving his family back to the States until the war blows over. Says he, "I've got no business fighting in a war. Why, I've got a wife and six little children. What would they do if I got kilt?" Willis stood up suddenly and says right to the man's face, "Well, if something ain't worth fighting and dying for, then I say it ain't worth having." He stomped off. Papa says, "Was I ever that young?" The neighbor says, "If wars were left up to old codgers like me and you, Aaron, I reckon armies would be put out of business."

I hope Papa is not planning on moving. I cannot bear to think of leaving my beautiful Texas.

Wednesday, January 13

Nothing happened all week. Just rain and chores. Folks say David Crockett is in east Texas and headed this way. Lem is very excited at the prospect of meeting his hero. I suppose they do have some things in common, both loving the woods and critters, but I don't think ol' Davy would hesitate killing a hog.

Saturday, January 16

Visited Mittie today. Since the sad news of her father's death, she doesn't talk much anymore. Mrs. Roe is thinking of moving back to Missouri, as she is a widow now. I cannot bear the thought of losing them.

At the store, we overheard a scout say that the citizens of San Antonio are starting to leave because they believe there is going to be a big battle there. Rumor has it that Santa Anna is on his way from Mexico with thousands of soldiers. Mittie's face turned white, then she ran home. When I told Mama, she didn't say much, but I know she is thinking about Uncle Isaac and that little baby who will be born soon.

Sunday, January 17

The Roes didn't come over today. It doesn't seem like the Sabbath at all.

Monday, January 18

Washed clothes, though it was drizzly and had to hang them up inside the house to dry. I've never seen so much confusion around town. Everyone is hearing conflicting stories. Scouts carrying messages keep coming and going through town. One said General Sam Houston ordered James Bowie to blow up the Alamo in San Antonio and have the men retreat here to Gonzales. Other rumors said Houston is not in charge. Nobody knows which end is up.

Tuesday, January 19

Rumors, rumors, rumors! I am so sick of rumors. The most frightening one is that General Santa Anna is already in northern Mexico. But Papa says that Santa Anna would have to be insane to march an army across the Mexican desert and mountains in the dead of winter with no food for the wagon train mules and cavalry horses. The weather is getting colder and those soldiers and pack animals would surely freeze to death.

Wednesday, January 20

It was too cold to go outside long. When I milked the cow, steam shot up from the milk pail and my fingers felt numb from the cold. The cow slapped my face with her tail. I had to tie it to the post with a piece of rope.

Thursday, January 21

After chores, I walked to town, though it was bitter cold. I saw Mittie in front of the Dickinson house shivering and looking all forlorn.

"I wish the Dickinsons hadn't left," Mittie said. "You know, Susanna didn't even say good-bye to us."

Though the Dickinsons left back in December, Mittie pouted and begin to sniff, saying she'd never see Susanna and Angelina again. I patted her shoulder and reassured her that all would be well. I am worried about her, though. Ever since she got word about her pa, every little thing gets her all upset and her mind seems to wander. Being around her is like walking on eggshells. I must think of something to cheer her up

Friday, January 22

I traded my Spanish candle to Mrs. McCoy for an old copy of *Ladies' Magazine*. When I gave the magazine to Mittie, she hugged my neck and squeezed my hand. Though the fashion sketches are old, Mittie studied them like they were the latest style in Philadelphia or New York City. It was so good to see her smile again and forget her troubles for a little while. I hope Willis forgives me for trading off his pretty candle.

Saturday, January 23

Today a message arrived from Uncle Isaac. It said:

> *Dearest Sister — Esperanza is too sick to be moved. The doctor says if she walks or gets upset, the baby will come too early. I refuse to leave her here, no matter how many Mexicans march through town. Sister, I implore you, <u>do not risk your life coming here. Stay in Gonzales</u>. Your devoted brother, Isaac*

Poor Mama. She twisted her apron into a tight little rope all the while I read the message. What she will do now, I do not know. Papa looked relieved.

Sunday, January 24

My heart is sad today. Just when I held hope that our lives might get back to normal, Willis announced that he is returning to San Antonio. Mama clamped her mouth shut and swallowed hard. I know she wanted to beg him to stay, but that isn't her way. She told me to start packing food and clothes. Papa told Willis to take one of the mules, but he declined. He said he didn't mind walking; besides Papa would need the mules to plow the fields come spring. Papa didn't say a word, but I know he was thinking what we were all thinking: Come spring, will there be fields to plow? Come spring, will there be a Texas?

I could not hold back my tears when Willis said good-bye to all of us. I gave him the biggest hug I could muster. Mama's chin quivered and I knew it wouldn't be long before she would go behind the smokehouse for a good cry.

★ ★ ★

Monday, January 25

We miss Willis already. Why does it always have to be the fine young men who go off to war? I asked Mama and she said that part of being a fine young man is being brave-hearted. I suppose I'm glad that Willis is brave, but I'd rather have him here. I can't stop thinking about that silly wishbone and him getting the short piece.

Tuesday, January 26

Two men came over and they commenced to arguing. One of them called Papa a "rotten, cowardly Tory" for not wanting to go to war. They shouted at each other until I had to leave.

I am now up in my favorite live oak tree, straddling a limb as fat as any horse. As I look across the rolling hills toward the beautiful Guadalupe River, I see tiny little bluebonnet plants popping up around the rocks. Come April they will be in full bloom, carpeting the prairies and hills. A redbird is chirping not far from here and a squirrel is fussing at me from above. Everything looks so peaceful and calm. How can there be a war hovering on the horizon only seventy-five miles away? Why can't

Santa Anna just leave the Texians alone and why can't the Texians just obey the Mexican laws?

I don't understand most of what the men were arguing about except for this one thing: Only a hundred and fifty of our boys are in San Antonio to defend the Alamo in case Santa Anna marches into Texas. And dear Willis is now one of them.

Wednesday, January 27

I am on my last pencil. The other two wore down to tiny stubs. I do not know what I will do when this one is gone. Ink is as scarce around here as paper.

We heard that David Crockett was seen at Washington-on-the-Brazos last Saturday. Now Lemuel is at the road all day long, keeping watch.

Thursday, January 28

Papa shot a wild beef. The meat was stringy and tough, so Mama sliced it paper thin and put the strips over a low fire to dry into jerky. There was tallow in the cow, so Mama made candles. While she melted down the tallow, I cut some cane stalks into long pieces. Mama poured the liquid into the hollow stalks while I held the cotton cords that served as wicks. I made a little Betty lamp by sticking a cotton cord in a gourd, filled it half way with sand, then poured oil over the top. It serves as a cheap lantern.

Friday, January 29

Green knocked over my Betty lamp and burned a hole in his quilt. Mama chased him with a hickory stick, but he got away. Lord, deliver me from that boy.

Saturday, January 30

Mama's in a powerful foul mood. I can't do anything right anymore. Neither can Green or Lem. At least they're boys and can sneak off somewhere and pretend to be working in the fields or the woods. I have to work next to Mama all day.

I have not seen Mittie in days. Have given up on getting lessons.

Sunday, January 31

I woke up to the sound of Mama and Papa arguing — a very rare occurrence. Mama was packing the big trunk. Papa was sitting on the side of the bed, looking miserable. Green and Lem woke up and came to the room, looking confused.

"Put your shoes on, children," Mama said. I knew she was serious then. We never wear shoes unless for an important occasion.

"What's wrong?" I asked.

"Mrs. Lawrence has decided to go to San Antonio," Papa said. "Neither tornado nor hurricane can stop her once her mind is made up. Do as she says."

Green and I leaped for joy and rushed to get on our shoes. But Lemuel dashed his fist against his leg and said, "Ah, M-Mama, you know D-Davy Crockett is due any t-time. Now, I-I-I'll miss m-meeting him."

Papa told him not to worry about ol' Davy and to hitch up the wagon. We loaded everything we might need, including the quilts, cornmeal, pork, an iron skillet, and an iron kettle. I wasn't sure if Papa was coming until the last minute when he climbed aboard and took the reins. I don't think Mama knew if he was coming until then, either. She sat there, her back rigid, her split bonnet shading her eyes as she stared straight ahead.

We stopped by the Roe house on the way out and Papa asked Mittie if she would feed our chickens and dogs while we were gone. Mrs. Roe shook her head and said, "Aaron and Rebecca, I hope you know what you're doing." Mittie bawled her eyes out and said she knew she would never see us alive again 'cause of Santa Anna. I laughed but my heart was pounding like a drum.

Monday, February 1

We traveled twelve miles yesterday, following the trail made by so many Volunteers and Texians coming and going the past few months. It is no more than a trail churned by cattle, but there are a few marked posts to guide us. Papa says it is a miracle any wagon can survive the trip.

We traveled only eight miles today, due to a stretch of muddy trail. Riding in the wagon is so rough that we all walk except for Papa. Every time the wheel hit a bump, I saw a grimace of pain on his face. At noon-time, while we broke to eat, Mama washed his face with a wet cloth that I had dipped in a creek. We rested two hours before moving on through the mud and cactus and rocks.

The campfire feels grand. My legs are aching from walking all day. Papa shot a rabbit and Mama is roasting it on a spit. The days are so short now, at this

rate of travel it will take us a week to get to Uncle
Isaac's.

Tuesday, February 2

Wagon axle broke. Papa and Lem have been working
on it all day. They are trying to make a new axle out of a
post oak tree they chopped down. I heard Mama say she
wished she had left alone on mule back; it would have
been faster.

Wednesday, February 3

The new axle didn't work properly so Papa says we
will have to abandon the wagon. He wants to go back
to Gonzales for help. Mama said she would ride a mule
the rest of the way to San Antonio alone while the rest
of us returned to Gonzales, but Papa told her she would
do no such thing; we will all stay together.

Drizzled all day. Mama prayed a long time. We are a
miserable lot.

Thursday, February 4

We abandoned our wagon and started walking back
toward Gonzales early this morning. Oh, how low our

spirits were, especially Mama's. We had only walked one mile when we met some men riding our way. The leader, dressed in buckskin, was very tall and well built, with friendly eyes, a pleasant smile, and a fiddle strapped to his back.

When Papa told him about our situation and the broken wagon, the man said, "Well, Mr. Lawrence, David Crockett has never turned his back on a man in need. Me and my Tennessee boys will be happy to help." Lemuel's mouth about hit the ground when he heard the words "David Crockett." He stood in his tracks like a frightened rabbit. I had to nudge him in the ribs to get him moving.

Mr. Crockett is the nicest man. He and his strong-shouldered friends had the wagon up and a new axle in the wheels before you could turn around. Mama cooked up some cornbread in hog grease, then cut big pieces of ham for all the men. They had hearty appetites and didn't seem to be in a hurry. Mr. Crockett said they had signed up with the Texas army and were on their way to San Antonio to join other Volunteers at the Alamo. He said that General Sam Houston had reports that part of the Mexican army was headed for Goliad south of here, and that the rest of the Mexican army was headed toward San Antonio, west of here.

Mama told Mr. Crockett that she had a brother in

Goliad, and another brother and a son in San Antonio. He leaned over and touched her hand.

Says Mr. Crockett in a kind voice, "I've never met a braver lot than Texian wives and mothers. Your long-suffering and gentle nature is what those sons and brothers and husbands are fighting for."

Mama took some comfort in his words. After lunch, Mr. Crockett took out his fiddle and played some merry tunes. He was right talented, I thought. We knew the words to some of the songs and we all clapped hands and sang along like it was a revival meeting. Lem never got his tongue and spent most of the time gawking at Mr. Crockett and never once asked him questions about bears and wildcats and such. Mr. Crockett told me I had the prettiest red hair he'd ever seen. Maybe he was joshing, but I will never forget him as long as I live and I must admit meeting him will probably be the high spot of my life.

Friday, February 5

Green keeps tormenting me with questions about Uncle Isaac's store. It is the only thing on his mind of late. He seems to think that Uncle Isaac will open the doors and let Green have his pick of goods.

Papa's leg is hurting fiercely. He can't find any

position that brings comfort. We lost three hours crossing a swollen creek today. I think Mama is beginning to regret this trip.

Saturday, February 6

The ground leveled off and we traveled a good distance. I am covered with dirt from head to toe; my shoes are down in the heels. Too weary to write.

Sunday, February 7

A beautiful day with bright sunshine! We saw many longhorned cattle on the hillsides, horses, sheep, and goats, too. Several Tejano families in wagons have met us as they flee San Antonio. They are friendly and seem concerned for us. They warn us not to go into town.

A handsome Tejano rancher wearing a big black *sombrero* on his head and silver spurs rode up on a beautiful, high-spirited white horse. He introduced himself as Señor Castillo and spoke English perfectly, with a most pleasing accent. He said he owns a *hacienda* not far away.

Many of the families in San Antonio are fleeing to ranches like his for they feel there is going to be a big battle in town and they do not want to be caught in the middle of it. When Mama told him about Uncle Isaac and Aunt Esperanza, Señor Castillo advised that they leave town, because Santa Anna will not be merciful to any Texians he captures, nor will he be sympathetic to a Tejano woman who has married an Anglo. Señor Castillo generously offered to let Uncle Isaac and Aunt Esperanza stay at his *hacienda,* which he said was large enough to accommodate many people. Papa thought it was a good idea and got directions to the ranch. Mama felt a lot better.

We arrived on a hill outside San Antonio at dusk and pitched camp. Mama is so eager to see if Uncle Isaac is well, that she could hardly be made to stop though it grew dark. I heard the tinkle of bells and saw a brown-skinned boy wearing a colorful striped *serape* herding some goats. I shouted: *"Buenas noches!"* He grinned and waved at me. We can see the lights of San Antonio in the distance, though it is several miles away. I am so excited I cannot sit still. My dear little pencil is half gone. I pray Uncle Isaac has another in his store.

Monday, February 8

I have never seen so many buildings! The whiteness of their walls glistens in the sunshine. I can see the tall bell towers of no less than three mission churches. In the distance, I can also see the mission they call the Alamo. Its chapel has no bell tower, or if ever it did, the roof must have fallen in. But the heavy doors and thick, white stone walls look strong. There are rows of little stone rooms beside the chapel. Papa says that is where the friars used to live when it was a mission. There are cannons perched on the walls now.

Later —

Late this afternoon, our wagon crossed the San Antonio River. Suddenly we were surrounded by houses and buildings. Some of the adobe walls are stained with dirt; some have colorful shutters and bright flowers spilling out of boxes. I've never seen so many people! Women wear the most colorful clothes such as bright wool shawls over cotton skirts and blouses. Every house seems to have a woman sweeping the yard. Children, chickens, and goats run everywhere. I counted ten burros pulling little two-wheeled carts loaded with goods. My eyes are fat from the feasting.

As we passed the town square, we heard music and shouting. There in the middle of it all, standing on a cart to make him higher than the others, was David

Crockett. As he spoke, loud cheers rose into the sky. We saw Willis in the crowd and Lemuel ran to join him. Then we saw Uncle Isaac and you never heard such yelling and yoo-hooing in your life. Mama climbed down and ran to give him a big hug. Uncle Isaac is a bear of a man, with shoulders broad enough to carry an ox. He picked Mama right up off the ground and twirled her around. Then he hurried over to the wagon and took me under one arm and Green under the other and twirled us around. He shook Papa's hand and announced in a loud voice that he was the proud father of a new baby boy. He had named his son George Washington, since it was nearing Washington's birthday. Mama laughed for the first time in I don't know when.

Tuesday, February 9

All of us, even Willis, are staying at Uncle Isaac's house. It is made of adobe and quite comfortable. Uncle Isaac is letting me use his bottle of ink and feather quill, for my pencil is almost a stub. I have not quite mastered the quill yet. I have splattered ink all over the page and my fingers are stained black. It is very slow going, for I must stop and dip the quill every few words. Uncle Isaac said he will try to find me a pencil.

The baby looks like a shriveled red plum. I regret saying it, but it is true. He was born too early and is not filled out yet. Mama fusses over him and says he is the handsomest baby boy she's ever seen. I'm glad her own sons did not hear her.

Aunt Esperanza is pale as death and too weak to lift her hand. But she managed a smile for Mama and me all the same. The last time I saw her she was beautiful, but now she reminds me of a rose whose petals have faded and are ready to fall. It breaks my heart to see her this way. The doctor just shakes his head. He doesn't speak English, but he doesn't have to for his opinion is written in his sad eyes.

Poor Aunt Esperanza has no family to watch over her. She is an orphan. Her mother died many years ago and her father, who was once wealthy, was killed by General Santa Anna's soldiers in the uprising in Zacatecas. That is why Aunt Esperanza never has anything nice to say about the general. Like all the Mexican people, she calls Santa Anna *El Presidente*.

★ ★ ★

Wednesday, February 10

Papa rested all day with his leg propped up. The servant, a plump woman named Silvia, treats him like a king. I think he is enjoying it very much. Mama finally got Esperanza to eat some soup. Her color is looking better.

Green, Lemuel, and I could hardly wait to visit Uncle Isaac's general store. There we met his business partner, Señor Ramirez. Like so many of the local men, he sports a thick black mustache. Señor Ramirez told us that we could each pick out a gift. We spent an hour looking and touching. It was such a hard decision. I settled on some brightly colored wool yarn. It will be useful for so many things. Mama can knit it into a shawl or scarf for Papa, and the scraps can be used to make hair bows for me and Mittie. Green embarrassed me with his greed, but finally chose a bag of licorice and hard candy, just as I expected. Lem took a leather pouch to wear around his neck. Señor Ramirez insisted that each of us also take something he called chicle. It is the resin of a tree, I think, and it chews and chews, never dissolving like food, and has a pleasant taste.

Uncle Isaac found some pencils for me.

Thursday, February 11

Silvia's husband, Rafael, drove Green, me, and Lem all over town in a donkey cart this morning. Rafael speaks choppy English with a heavy accent, but after a while I got used to it and understood him, mostly. He knows who lives in every building and whose daughter married who, and which man had built which house. He showed us the houses where the battle had taken place back in December. Bullet holes dented the sides of the walls, cannonballs left big holes in roofs and front doors, and fighting men had knocked out large hunks of walls in some of the nicest houses. What a shame war destroys beautiful things.

Most of the women and girls go barefooted or wear sandals woven from yucca fibers. I never saw so many pretty young women. Their ruffled skirts swished as they walked by. Music and loud laughter came from taverns, called *cantinas,* though it was the middle of the day.

On the way home I saw a familiar figure walking down the street. It was Susanna Dickinson, carrying Angelina. Susanna was happy to see us. Angelina cooed and held her hands out to me. The Dickinsons are staying with the family of an important government official, Señor Musquiz. She invited us for supper tomorrow. I cannot wait to see the inside of that beautiful house.

Friday, February 12

For the fancy dinner, Mama ironed my best dress. I washed and combed my hair, and put a piece of blue yarn in it. The Musquiz house was glowing with candlelight when we arrived. It is the most beautiful house I've ever seen. The furniture is dark and massive, with intricate flowers carved on the table legs. The chairs have such high backs that even I felt small when sitting. Heavy wax candles dripped in huge candelabras.

Just before dinner I heard a familiar voice and saw David Crockett walk through the door. Beside him was a dashing man dressed in fine clothing and speaking Spanish fluently. On his belt hung a huge, broadbladed knife. Willis whispered into my ear that the man was James Bowie, whose reputation as an expert knife fighter follows him wherever he goes. He was dashing and courteous, and had the manners of a fine southern gentleman, but he drank too much wine. The food was delicious. We had bread made from wheat flour, not coarse cornmeal. I sipped my first wine and promptly choked on it.

As expected, the conversation soon turned to Santa

Anna and the war. There are about one hundred and fifty Anglos left in San Antonio, mostly Volunteers from the States, like David Crockett and his Tennessee boys. Several hundred Volunteers went south to the presidio at Goliad, where Uncle Henry is. The original Texians who gathered at Gonzales back in October have returned home to work their farms, for it will soon be time to plant crops.

Susanna said, "The poor Volunteers are in dirty, tattered clothes. They have not been paid yet and cannot even afford the cost of getting clothes washed."

"They may be dirty, but they'll stand and fight when the time comes, ma'am," Mr. Crockett said. "Our biggest problem is figuring out who is in command. Some say Jim here; others say that young lawyer, Bill Travis. Boys, we've got to stop this bickering and stick together or the Mexicans will stomp us into the ground."

At the mention of Travis's name, Col. Bowie's face turned red and he made some very unsavory remarks about that "hot-headed redhead." I was glad when the men retired to a room with a blazing fireplace and lit up cigars.

Rafael drove us home in the donkey cart. Along the way, we heard guitar music and laughter and shouting coming from *cantinas.* Through open doors I saw a beautiful Mexican girl dancing to fast music. Her skirt twirled, revealing ruffled petticoats. Her long black hair fell around her dark eyes and her hands clicked small wooden instruments that Rafael says are called *castañetas.* She reminded me of a cat, so limber and graceful. The guitars strummed louder and the *castañetas* clicked faster and her legs spun around and around until I was dizzy. Suddenly the music stopped and everyone cheered. I can still hear the music of guitars coming through the windows.

Saturday, February 13

Aunt Esperanza's health is much improved. Uncle Isaac is so happy, he can't sit still. He said as soon as Aunt Esperanza and the baby are strong enough, he will take them to the *hacienda* of Señor Castillo, who we met on the road. Papa says we will go back home soon, for it is time to plant corn.

Silvia took me, Green, and Lem to the marketplace today. It looked like the whole town was there buying or trading goods. It was like a big general store, only everything was outside. Silvia said that today's market was not half as large as usual because so many people have fled town and others are afraid to leave their houses because of the unruly Volunteers wandering the streets. Lem said not to worry, it's too early for them to be awake, and we all laughed. Silvia traded some big fat onions from her garden for a nice melon. She bought dried corn, yucca roots, dried red peppers, cactus pads with the needles picked off, and a basket of dried beans. I chewed more *chicle* until my jaw was sore.

When we got home, Silvia showed me how to make *tortillas* by forming a paste of cornmeal and water, rolling little balls, then patting them out with my hands. She also showed me how to make *tamales* by spreading cornmeal paste into dry corn husks, then putting in some meat and spices, then cooking the husks. Papa loves Silvia's hot, spicy cooking. Lem, Willis, Papa, and Uncle Isaac had a hot-pepper-eating contest. Willis won, then ran down to the river and dipped his face in the water.

Sunday, February 14

The church bells began ringing very early this morning. Silvia, dressed in her black dress and black shawl, invited me to attend Mass. I was surprised

Mama said yes and let Silvia tie a lacy scarf around my head.

San Fernando church is huge, made from massive stones. It has a tall bell tower and the bell is so loud it sounds all over the town. The priests greeted people outside the door. The women wore their best. The rich ones sat at the front, wearing silks and lace and head-coverings called *mantillas*. I have never seen such lovely clothing. The poorer folks, like Silvia and Rafael, sat farther back, wearing mostly plain cotton clothes and sandals. The head priest spoke Latin so I didn't understand a word he said. He didn't jump up and down and stomp and spit like a Methodist minister. The singing was beautiful. Though I didn't understand, I was almost moved to tears. I wish Mittie could have heard it.

After Mass, Silvia and Rafael spoke to several friends. I don't know what they said, but I heard the word Santa Anna many times and their faces looked worried. When we got home, Silvia said to Uncle Isaac, "Santa Anna has reached the Rio Grande with his army. He will be in San Antonio in a week."

Uncle Isaac dismissed the news with a wave of his hand. Says he, "It's just another rumor being spread by Santa Anna's spies. They're everywhere. Santa Anna can't get here that fast. Besides that, it's winter. There's no food for the horses and mules." But a chill ran up my spine anyway. Suppose it's not a rumor. Suppose it is true.

Monday, February 15

I accompanied Silvia to the San Antonio River, which flows beside the town. We washed clothes right in the water, scrubbing them with our hands. Many women were doing the same thing. They talked and laughed like it was a party. I recognized one of the girls as the dancer from the *cantina*. I asked Mama if I could have a ruffled red petticoat and she said a decent girl had no need of ruffles.

Tuesday, February 16

Papa's leg is better, though he still uses crutches. He took the wagon to a wheelwright and had the axle repaired good and proper. He said we will be leaving for home soon. Baby Washington is getting stronger. His little face is plump and the wrinkles are gone. He's adorable now, with his big black eyes and dark hair. Uncle Isaac is calling him Wash for short. As soon as

Aunt Esperanza can walk, Wash will be christened. Then we leave. I love this charming town, but I surely do not want to be here if the Mexican army arrives.

Wednesday, February 17

Papa wanted to test the sturdiness of the new wagon axle, so we drove Willis out to the Alamo across the river on the outskirts of town. Up close, the old mission is much smaller than I thought it would be. It is encroached upon by a small village, La Villita, made up of dozens of poorly constructed stick houses called *jacales.* Only a few men were at the Alamo being drilled by William Travis. The rest, I am told, are staying in town with Tejano families. The engineer was supervising the making of dirt ramps for loading cannons.

Almeron Dickinson was repairing one of the cannons left behind by the Mexican general. David Crockett was busy building a temporary wall of earth located next to the chapel. One man was carving out holes in the barracks to make slots for the guns. It was a very warm day, and the men were sweating profusely. I was so glad to hear that Col. Travis and Col. Bowie have finally settled their squabble and agreed to share the command.

Thursday, February 18

Another warm day. Aunt Esperanza felt well, so we accompanied her to the church of San Fernando to have little Wash christened. He was so sweet, dressed in his white gown with elaborate lace and embroidery. Wash cooed and didn't cry, even when the priest sprinkled water on his head and it trickled down his cheeks. Aunt Esperanza and Uncle Isaac were beaming with pride, and a lot of people came over for dinner afterwards. By the end of the day, my aunt was exhausted.

It is late and everyone is asleep. Just now I was about to blow out the candle and retire to my room when there was a knock at the back door and a lot of excited talk in Spanish. Silvia woke up Uncle Isaac and said, *"El Presidente* crossed the Rio Grande on Tuesday with two thousand soldiers and is now only four days away from San Antonio. You must leave, *Señor.* It is too dangerous for you and *la señora."*

But Uncle Isaac said, "It's just more rumors spread by Santa Anna's spies. Remember, some men claimed to have spotted Santa Anna crossing the Rio Grande two weeks ago and that was false. Don't worry, Silvia, we still have until spring. Go back to sleep." Silvia whispered a stream of Spanish, then made the sign of the cross before returning to her quarters.

Friday, February 19

Uncle Isaac is boiling mad. Silvia and Rafael packed up and left in the middle of the night. Now there is no one to cook or clean or help with the baby, except for Mama and me. Mama got out the cornmeal and made a big pan of cornbread and cut up some ham. Aunt Esperanza hardly ate a bite and cried all morning. Silvia had been her servant for fifteen years and was like a mother to her.

Aunt Esperanza is sure that Santa Anna will march into town any day now and she wants to leave immediately. Uncle Isaac says she is not well enough yet. They argued and he left, fuming mad. He doesn't trust the Mexicans who brought the news, but Aunt Esperanza says that El Presidente is not one to sit back and take insult. She knows in her heart that he is planning revenge and will show no mercy to the Texians and their Tejano friends. I am getting nervous.

At supper time, Willis said there is to be a big fandango to celebrate George Washington's birthday on Monday evening. Papa said it appears to him there has been a fandango every night and a fiesta every day. Willis assures us that this one is going to be especially big. I asked Mama if I might attend and she said only if Lem and Green can go along, too. It's a poor bargain, but I accepted.

Saturday, February 20

Aunt Esperanza gave Mama material from one of her old silk dresses to make me a new ensemble for the fandango. It is the most beautiful cloth I have ever seen, soft and smooth, not like the wrinkled homespun I'm used to. Mama worked on it all day while I did the chores and cooking. I made flour biscuits. Aunt Esperanza said they were delicious, but the men all laughed and said they might come in handy as targets for gun practice. Lem said they would make good filling for chinks in the cabin as they surely appeared to be waterproof. Only Willis said they were right tasty, though I saw him wink at Uncle Isaac. No matter. I endured their teasing because Mama was busy in a back room sewing my beautiful dress.

★ ★ ★

Sunday, February 21

Aunt Esperanza attended Mass early in the morning and everyone made a big fuss over little Wash. I saw Susanna Dickinson riding in the Musquiz family's carriage and she gave me a ride. It was my first carriage ride. How smooth and flawless it felt as the wheels rolled over the stone streets. So much better than the rough wagon. The horse was beautiful, with a small delicate head and high-stepping legs. Susanna said she will be at the fandango and is looking forward to it. She asked me which young man I wanted to dance with and anxiety struck my heart. I never thought of it until that very moment. Now I can think of nothing else. If Galba were here, there would be no question, but he is in Gonzales. The rain is pounding the roof now. Please, do not rain tomorrow night.

Monday, February 22

Happy Birthday, Mr. George Washington! And thank you, Lord, for clearing the skies in time for the fandango. Mama finished up my dress just in time and I must say it is beautiful, though I was disappointed that she left off the ruffles. I peered at myself in the mirror until Mama said I was acting like Mittie Roe. I got dressed much too early and felt all tingly waiting for the evening to arrive. Mama, Papa, and Aunt Esperanza stayed home. My brothers, Uncle Isaac, and I walked to the party, our spirits as high as the moon.

The light poured out into the night, and the guitar and fiddle music was loud enough to stir the dead. David Crockett played his fiddle merrily, Tejanos strummed their mellow guitars, and a Scotsman blew his squealing bagpipes until everyone covered their ears. The food was delicious and the laughter and noise riotous. Willis danced with me two times, to loosen up his step, he said. I tried to get Lem to dance, but he said he'd rather get bit by a skunk than dance with a girl. Green was willing, though, so I taught him every step I knew to the Virginia reel, the cotillion, and the waltz. A German man showed me and Susanna how to dance the polka, which was so lively I thought my heart was going to burst. Most of the Mexican women didn't know the steps, but the rough Texians dragged them across the floor anyway, hooting and hollering. I have never attended so grand a party and could not believe how swiftly time passed.

There were no boys my age, so most of my dances were with Green, Willis, or Uncle Henry. How I wished that Galba was there.

Around eleven o'clock, I spied a boy about sixteen years old looking at me from across the room. He came over and introduced himself as James Allen, then asked for a dance. We danced five times! What a wonderful dancer he is. We talked a right smart. I fibbed and said I was fourteen and prayed the good Lord didn't strike me down with lightning. James said I was mature for my age. I will write the next thing that happened very small so that no one will see it. He kissed me. I think he said, "You are very pretty," but my heart was pounding in my ears so loud I can't be sure. Then Lem ran up and said we had to go right away. James squeezed my hand and said he hoped to see me around.

I wanted to stay, oh, how I wanted to stay and dance some more, but we had promised Mama to be home by midnight. The fandango was still going strong as we left. I saw a Tejano talking excitedly to David Crockett and William Travis. They had worried looks on their faces.

I arrived at Uncle Isaac's house expecting to find all asleep, but every candle and lamp was lit. Papa's wagon was piled with furniture and belongings, and so was the little donkey cart. It was the same all over town. Every house was a flurry of activity. This time there was no mistaking the messengers: Santa Anna and his soldiers were camped at the Medina River only eight miles west of town. Had it not been for the sudden heavy rain of yesterday, he would have already been here.

I ran inside and Papa shouted at us for being so late and asked where Willis was. We told him Willis was still at the fandango. While Papa and Uncle Isaac nailed boards over the windows and locked the garden gates, Mama and Aunt Esperanza and I packed food, clothes, bed linens, and silverware.

It is now four o'clock in the morning. Mama has just said to put up my diary and get into bed as we will leave early. I will finish my story when I can.

Tuesday, February 23

All night long we heard the rumble of carts and wagons as citizens fled the town. We awoke late and found that the donkey was gone. We had to remove everything from the cart and take some things out of the wagon and leave them behind. This took a while. Mama was very upset, as the donkey cart was going to serve as a bed for Aunt Esperanza and the baby. Willis was still not back and Mama refused to leave without him.

It was after lunch before we found Willis. Mama shouted, "The Mexicans are upon us, Willis. Climb into the wagon!" But Willis shook his head and said, "It's just another rumor started by Santa Anna's spies."

The words were hardly out of his mouth when the bells of San Fernando church started ringing wildly. Everyone stopped and turned toward the church whose white steeple rose above the trees and the rows of adobe houses. All of a sudden Volunteers began running for the Alamo across the river on the outskirts of town. "The Mexican army is here!" Their cries filled the air up and down the streets.

Willis grabbed his rifle and slung it over his shoulder. "I guess you are right this time," he said, grinning.

Papa took Willis's arm and said, "Son, it's foolish to stay. They outnumber you ten to one. Don't you know that?"

But Willis shook his head and said, "I'm not worried, Papa. The Alamo is strong. If we can stall Santa Anna here for a few days, the rest of Texas will have time to rally."

"But why does it have to be *you* who stays?" I cried out and hugged him with all my heart.

Willis tweaked my nose and said, "Because, if I ran away, I'd never be able to look you in the eyes again, Cinda." He smiled. "Don't worry. We've whipped the Mexicans before, and we'll whip 'em again."

Mama's eyes filled with tears as she pushed her

favorite handkerchief into Willis's hand and told him to pray every night. I gave him the yarn from my hair and he tied it around his rifle barrel. Uncle Isaac held Baby Wash real close, like he was smelling him, then kissed him and placed him in Aunt Esperanza's arms. He said something to her in Spanish and her eyes got real big. She screamed and began weeping hysterically. Uncle Isaac had to tear himself away. He kissed Mama, shook Papa's hand, then put on his hat and he and Willis joined the other running men.

We watched Uncle Isaac and Willis running down the street toward the footbridge that crossed the San Antonio River. Papa had a funny look in his eyes and when he turned to Mama, she said in a firm voice, "Don't you think of it, Mr. Lawrence. You have a family that needs you. The Texians don't want an old cripple-leg like you. You can help them better by getting word back to the colonies." It seemed like forever before Papa heaved a sigh, slammed his hat over his brow, and climbed up in the wagon. He shook the reins and cracked the loose ends over the poor mules' backs.

Later —

We are now camped many miles east of San Antonio. Earlier, as we left town and passed near the Alamo,

I saw some Tejano women and children taking refuge in the old mission. Just before the gates closed, a horse charged in. Seated behind the rider was a pretty young woman with dark hair, holding a little girl in her arms. It was Susanna Dickinson and little Angelina. She was keeping her promise. My heart felt sick at the sight.

By four o'clock we had cleared La Villita outside town and were approaching our first hill when we heard loud cheers from the town and voices shouting, *"Viva México! Viva El Presidente!"* Drums pounded and bugles sounded clear, sharp notes. Papa urged the mules faster and they broke into a little trot. I turned around and saw a sight that made my heart stop — row after row of Mexican soldiers marching down the street. The sun glistened off their bright uniforms, some red and blue, others all white, and their fixed bayonets. At the head of the column rode officers on prancing horses. One horse had an arched tail that shined like corn silk. The small man sitting erect on its back wore a glorious uniform and his sword scabbard twinkled. Surely it was General Santa Anna himself.

I tried to count the soldiers, but it was hopeless. As we crested a second, higher hill, I saw that the line of soldiers extended westward from town. And across the San Antonio River, in an empty prairie, the little white Alamo stood alone like David against a thousand Goliaths.

We heard a big boom and saw smoke from the eighteen-pounder cannon atop the Alamo wall. In the town plaza, a soldier hoisted the red, white, and green Mexican flag and then another flag, blood-red in color, from the top of the San Fernando church steeple. Green asked Papa what the red flag meant, but he didn't reply. Lem whispered in my ear these chilling words: "It m-means no q-quarter; every m-man in the Alamo w-will be put to d-death."

It is dark now. Two messengers have just galloped by carrying a plea from Col. Travis for reinforcements. I wonder how many men will come to his aid.

Wednesday, February 24

This morning we were awakened by the sound of steady cannonade from the direction of San Antonio and we knew the Alamo was besieged. With each distant boom, my heart ached for dear Willis and Uncle Isaac, for Susanna, and for everyone inside the old mission. The cannonade lasted all day long. Every time we heard the loudest boom, that of the eighteen-pounder in the Alamo, Papa would say, "The Alamo still stands."

We camped in a live oak grove. Papa says Señor Castillo's ranch is only a few miles away. During the night, we heard thundering horse hooves and Papa grabbed his old pistol. It was yet another express courier on his way from the Alamo. While he rested his horse and drank a cup of coffee, I read the message to everyone by the light of the campfire:

To The People of Texas and all Americans <u>in the</u> <u>*World*</u>

Fellow citizens & Compatriots —

I am besieged by a thousand or more of the Mexicans under Santa Anna — I have sustained a continual Bombardment & cannonade for 24 hours & have not lost a man — The enemy has demanded a surrender at discretion, otherwise, the garrison are to be put to the sword, if the fort is taken — I have answered the demand with a cannon shot, & our flag still waves proudly from the walls — <u>I shall never surrender or</u> <u>retreat.</u> Then, I call on you in the name of Liberty, of patriotism & every thing dear to the American character, to come to our aid, with all dispatch — The enemy is receiving reinforcements daily & will no doubt increase to three or four thousand in four or five days. If this call is neglected, I am determined to sustain myself

as long as possible & die like a soldier who never forgets
what is due to his own honor & that of his country —
<u>*VICTORY OR DEATH*</u>
William Barret Travis
Lt. Col. Comdt.

The messenger said he planned to round up some men and supplies in Gonzales and return to the Alamo. Mama told him to take whatever meat was in our smokehouse. Papa said he would join the men as soon as he had dropped off Aunt Esperanza and got his family back home. Mama has been silent since.

Thursday, February 25

We reached the *hacienda* before noon and unloaded the wagon. Señor Castillo and several friends were on their way to join Captain Juan Seguín, a polite and intelligent landowner who is the leader of the Tejanos fighting against Santa Anna. The spacious house has a courtyard in the middle with a well and flowers. Servants bustled everywhere and fat livestock grazed on the hillsides. Señor Castillo invited all of us to stay there, but only Aunt Esperanza accepted his offer. She felt safe there and wanted to stay as close to San

Antonio as possible, where Uncle Isaac is. Though Papa's leg was hurting from all the jostling, he insisted on leaving immediately.

As the day progressed, the weather changed. By afternoon an evil-looking squall line rolled in the distance, signifying a blue norther. The storm struck with fury and the temperature dropped to almost freezing. We are now huddled inside our wagon in the middle of the woods. The north wind howls like a demon and so do the wolves out on the prairie. We heard the booming eighteen-pounder, though more faintly now. Green cheered and shouted, "The Alamo still stands!" My fingers are too cold to write more tonight.

Friday, February 26

A cold miserable day as we crossed a stretch of open prairie. We children huddled in the back of the wagon under the quilt but couldn't get warm. It was too cold to stop and cook, so all we ate all day was cold, tough beef jerky. We are still many miles from Gonzales. Papa is anxious to keep going, but Mama said there is no use in busting an axle on some unseen rock or hole. I hope that Willis is warm.

Saturday, February 27

Another bitter cold day with a strong north wind. It was hardly above freezing when we awoke. Papa's leg was so stiff he could not walk. Mama built a fire and warmed the blanket and wrapped it around Papa's leg, then she and Lem lifted him up onto the wagon. Mama took the reins herself.

It warmed up some during the day but the wind did not cease. In the evening we came across a group of men pitching camp. Nearly all of them were Gonzales men.

The leader said they had organized as soon as they received the first message from Travis and were headed for the Alamo. I saw three boys no older than sixteen. I was dismayed that one of them was Galba. He smiled and asked me where Willis was. I told him he was in the Alamo. I handed Galba the blue ribbon from my diary and asked him to carry it for good luck. That pleased him. My heart is sick, sick, sick. Mama asked me to write down all the names of the men, in case someone needs to know later on. They are:

Isaac Baker; John Cane; George Cottle; Jacob Darst; Squire Daymon; William Deardruff; William Fishbaugh; John Flanders; D. W. Floyd; Galba Fuqua;

John Garvin; John Gaston (who sometimes goes by his stepfather's last name, Davis); James George; Thomas Jackson; Johnnie Kellog, who is only nineteen; Andrew Kent; George Kimball; William King; Albert Martin; Jesse McCoy; Thomas Miller, the richest man in town; Isaac Millsaps (I can't believe he went off and left his blind wife and seven children behind); George Neggan; William Summers; George Tumlinson; Robert White; Claiborne Wright. There were also some men who don't live in Gonzales, but were traveling with them: David Cummings from Pennsylvania; Jonathan Lindley, a land surveyor; Charles Despallier, who is a friend of Travis; and the redhead, John Smith, who is guiding them to San Antonio.

Papa decided to drive on home, though it was dark. When we got to the house, Mama and Lem had to carry him from the wagon. Blood stained his pants where the wound had reopened. Papa is suffering, but I think Mama is relieved. With his leg hurting so bad, surely he will not return to San Antonio.

We were too tired to eat supper. It feels good to be home, but everyone is strangely quiet. Green dragged his mattress into the room and put it beside mine again.

★ ★ ★

Sunday, February 28

Another cold day. Papa was too sick to get up, though he tried. When Mama told him that the mules were too exhausted to move, he finally fell back in bed. Though he is against the war, he still feels it is his duty to help.

First thing this morning after chores, I ran to Mittie's house. We hugged and cried like babies. I gave her some colored yarn and a piece of the *chicle* to chew. I told her all about San Antonio, the Alamo, and the Mexican army. Mrs. Roe led us in a prayer for our boys. Hearing it made me so sad I had to leave. I forgot to tell Mittie about James Allen and my first kiss. I am glad to be among my friends, but the town does not look right anymore. There are only a few men left, and most are old or crippled like Papa. Another convention is to be held March 1 at Washington-on-the-Brazos.

Monday, February 29

Leap year day. Some say it is a bad omen. Papa got up early and saddled a mule. He said he was going to San Antonio, despite his bad leg. Mama begged him to stay. When Papa said Texas needed him, Mama broke loose and yelled, "Texas! I've already given a baby daughter, a son, and two brothers for Texas. When is the good Lord going to say enough?" Then she ran behind the smokehouse.

Papa looked miserable and didn't say a word for a long time. Lem took the reins and said, "P-P-Papa? I'll go in your p-p-place." Papa looked shocked, then he hugged Lem real tight and his eyes got all watery. I do believe that is the first time I ever saw Papa look at Lem with pride in his eyes. He cleared his throat and says, "No, Lemuel, you stay here. I think even the Lord draws the line at sending a fifteen-year-old boy into battle."

Tonight is bitter cold. The sky is clear and I see a million brilliant stars. I can't help but think about Halley's Comet that we saw back in October before all this war business started. All I wanted back then was to dance with Galba and have a red hair ribbon. How senseless and childish those things seem now. As I pull my shawl around my shoulders, I think of Willis behind those cold, cold mission walls. And what about our town's men who just left to answer Col. Travis's call for help? How will they ever get through the lines of Mexican soldiers? Oh, how I wish this war had never started.

Tuesday, March 1

Lemuel is gone. His pet raccoon and pet crow are missing, too. Mama thinks he has gone off to fight at the Alamo and the thought of it is weighing her shoulders down. She sank into her rocking chair, so I started the fire and cooked breakfast myself. Afterwards, I walked to Mittie's house. It was almost too cold to go, but I was glad I did because she and Mrs. Roe helped me look for Lem. We walked up and down the river calling his name. No one has seen him all day. I assured Mama that he was just looking for honey, but she does not believe me. Green was gone all day looking in the woods. Papa told Mama he would stay in Gonzales after all. I am weary of worrying about men and their wars. If it were not for my dear diary, surely I would lose all sense.

Wednesday, March 2

Still no sign of Lemuel. Mama has accepted that he must have gone to the Alamo, though being on foot it will take him days to get there. An express rider going from Goliad to San Felipe passed through town. He changed horses and handed out some letters from the men at Goliad. Mama received one from Uncle Henry. After I read it, I almost wished I had not. It says:

Dearest Sister and family:

We are unable to leave because our horses were confiscated last month by Col. Johnson. Now, we just received word that all Johnson's men were killed in a surprise attack by the Mexicans at San Patricio. Any who surrendered were killed, as is the policy of Santa Anna toward all Texians, who he considers to be traitors to Mexico.

Day before yesterday we set out with about three hundred men afoot and four pieces of artillery in wagons to aid the men in the Alamo. We had no beef, no bread, and very little ammunition. One wagon broke down right outside town, and it took us all day to get the artillery across the river. The officers held a council of war and decided to wait until more supplies arrived, as it was not wise to leave the presidio here unprotected. There is word that part of the Mexican army is headed this way. The boys have named our presidio Fort Defiance. We are determined to defend it to the last man, for if the Mexicans break through here, they will be in the colonies in no time, ravaging our homes. My heart prays for the men in the Alamo, but as you can see, we have our own problems. If more Texians do not come to our aid, all will be lost.

If the Mexican army breaks through, help Nancy and the children get back to the States. This may be the last letter I write. My love to all of you. Please send this message on to Nancy. For God and Liberty,

Your brother, Henry

I am glad there was no more to the letter, for the big lump in my throat would not let me read another word.

Thursday, March 3

I saw Lem's raccoon today. I know it was Bandit for he was standing on his haunches and waving his hands like a little beggar. He let me pick him up and ate corn right from my hand. I didn't tell Mama, as we all know that Lem would never leave Bandit behind unless it was a serious emergency.

I took Bandit to the Roes and asked Mittie to keep him tied up a few days. Mrs. Roe wasn't too pleased, but she promised not to tell Mama. I cannot imagine where Lem is. He hates killing any living thing; I know he could not kill a man.

Mama does not talk about Lem, Willis, Uncle Isaac, or Uncle Henry. She hitched up the mules to the plow today and began furrowing the fields. She says work is the only thing that helps her. For me it is this diary that calms my soul.

Friday, March 4

I saw a broadside posted on the front window of the general store. It was composed by Gen. Sam Houston himself. It said, "The citizens of Texas must rally to the aid of our army, or it will perish." The notice claimed that every able-bodied man in Texas was expected to join in the fight against the Mexicans. Any men seen heading east, away from the war, will be considered deserters and their weapons confiscated and given to the Texas army. If a family decides to leave on account of the war only one man is allowed to escort it out of Texas.

Saturday, March 5

The day opened clear and cool. I helped Mama plow, as it is past time to get the corn and cotton seeds into the ground. An express courier passed through on his way to Washington-on-the-Brazos with a message from Col. Travis at the Alamo. The messenger said Col. Travis will fire the eighteen-pounder cannon every morning, noon, and evening as long as he can. Around noon, Green climbed a hill west of town to listen for the distant faint booms. Then he ran back home and announced in a loud, clear voice, "The Alamo still stands." Papa says it is just Green's imagination, but the hope and faith of that innocent child help to keep us going.

Sunday, March 6

A division of Mexican soldiers killed another company of Texians not far from Goliad, where Uncle Henry is garrisoned. The news shook Mama terribly.

Over two hundred men have gathered in Gonzales, mostly Texian farmers. They are fortifying the town by chopping trees and building palisades. Not every man agrees on what to do. Some want to help the boys at the Alamo instead of staying here.

Papa helps by driving our wagon to haul logs, rocks, and so forth. He feels much better now, knowing he is helping the cause, even though he was opposed to the war in the first place. He says now he has to fight, whether he likes it or not, because he is protecting his family and land. He says that keeping busy helps to take his mind off Willis and Lemuel. He also says if Lem is just hiding out someplace, he will skin him alive when he finds him.

Monday, March 7

We are very worried. There has been no message from Col. Travis since the one dated March 3. Still no word from Lemuel. Mama says surely any Mexicans who might capture Lem would not consider him guilty of treason, being only a child. All of us agreed with her. What else could we do?

We finished plowing the cornfield and got the seeds in the ground. We must plow the cotton fields next.

Tuesday, March 8

Glory hallelujah! *Texas has declared her independence!* Word has just arrived. The convention delegates at Washington-on-the-Brazos met in a half-built building on March 2, during that awful cold norther. They had no fire or anything to keep them warm. Maybe that is why they acted so fast and made the declaration so short. Mrs. Roe and I gathered all the scraps of paper we could find and transcribed copies to give to messengers to spread to the other settlements. I will memorize the words to tell my grandchildren when I am old and gray.

Wednesday, March 9

Though the temperature is mild, a violent wind blows. It knocks us over as we walk. Two strapping big Volunteers saw Mama trying to plow and took over for her. They had the cotton field finished by the end of the day. Mama cooked them the best meal she could scrape together. They promised to come back to help plant the cotton seeds. My faith in the Volunteers is restored.

We are sick with worry. No one has heard the eighteen-pounder cannon since Sunday morning, not even a scouting party coming in from San Antonio. Papa said maybe Col. Travis is saving powder. I pray he is right.

Thursday, March 10

Green came in from town very excited. Gen. Sam Houston has sent orders for all able-bodied men in Texas to gather at Gonzales for the purpose of rescuing the Alamo. The men at Goliad are to come here, too. All told, that will make about one thousand men ready and eager to fight. Gen. Houston will be here soon. We are very excited at the prospect of meeting him, as he has quite a reputation for being highly unusual in manner and in dress. Our hopes have rallied more than ever.

Friday, March 11

I was in town around four in the afternoon when much excitement commenced over the arrival of Gen. Sam Houston. He is a giant in stature, standing a head higher then most others. His legs seemed too long for the horse he rode. Wearing a Cherokee coat, buckskin vest, and broad-brimmed hat with a feather in it, he would have looked more like a frontiersman than a commander in chief, were it not for his fine pistol and fancy sword.

Hardly had the general dismounted, when two Tejano *rancheros* arrived from a *hacienda* near San Antonio. The ranchers claimed they had witnessed the defeat of the Americans in the Alamo. Gen. Houston accused them of being spies for Santa Anna and had them promptly arrested. He told us not to spread the rumor for it had not been confirmed. When I got home Papa said not to let Mama know yet. No need to have her worry needlessly.

A deep, dark gloom has settled over the town. Even the restless men camped nearby are very quiet and speak only in whispers when they gather in little groups on street corners. Everyone is waiting for the news of the Alamo. My common sense tells me all must be lost, but my heart still clings to hope.

Rumors are flying. If the Alamo has fallen, then four thousand Mexican soldiers are headed for Gonzales. Santa Anna has vowed to pillage and burn every Texian house and barn along the way. He will murder any Texian he finds and liberate the slaves. Such is the nature of Santa Anna. After destroying Gonzales, he will march onward to San Felipe and then to all the other colonies in Texas. We are counting heart and soul on Gen. Houston to stop Santa Anna at the Guadalupe River. But how can a few hundred poorly armed farmers defeat one of the largest and greatest armies in the world?

Saturday, March 12

The Roes left today. My heart ached with grief as we all hugged and said a tearful good-bye. Mittie gave me her red hair ribbon, and though I really do not care about ribbons anymore, I thanked her. We promised to keep in touch and reunite when this war is over.

As there has been no bad news from Goliad, we believe that Uncle Henry is still alive and well. A few days ago, Captain Juan Seguín, who leads the Tejanos fighting for Texas, sent two of his scouts to find out about the Alamo. But they have been gone too long and it is feared they have been captured and put to death for being spies.

Papa took apart his old pistol and oiled it. He has no more than five roughly made bullets and hardly enough powder. Such is the case with all the men. But they are determined to stop Santa Anna at the river. I prayed three times today — for Willis and Uncle Isaac and Uncle Henry. Even if the Alamo did fall, couldn't some of the men have escaped in the confusion?

Sunday, March 13

My fingers tremble as I write, and I must pause to wipe the tears from my eyes. But I must record this most horrible of days; it is the least I can do to honor the dead. Late this evening our worst fears were confirmed. Willis is dead. Uncle Isaac is dead. Dear, sweet

Galba, and those other boys, all dead. Nineteen-year-old Johnnie Kellog, whose young wife is due to deliver their first child any day; old Mr. Millsaps, whose blind widow has seven little children to raise alone; Mr. Miller, owner of the general store — all are dead. Col. Travis will never write in his journal again; James Bowie will never twirl his knife; David Crockett will never play his fiddle, nor spin a yarn.

Two of Houston's scouts met Susanna Dickinson and Angelina coming down the road today. Accompanying her was Joe, the black servant of William Travis, and Ben, a black servant of one of the Mexican generals, who carried a message from Santa Anna. Susanna's dress was sooty and grimy and her face was pale. She looked so old and tired, no longer a pretty young girl. Her blue eyes were full of the deepest pain one can imagine. She was taken straight away to Gen. Houston. A crowd gathered around while she told him what had happened.

She said she and several Tejano women and children had hidden in the Alamo sacristy during the thirteen days of the siege. The final attack came before dawn on Sunday, March 6. Cannons bombarded the old mission walls and the smoke from guns made the air thick and hard to breathe. The screams of thousands of attacking Mexican soldiers and the groans of dying and wounded men surrounded her. She feared that even she and the children would be put to the sword. Her brave husband had but a few seconds to tell her good-bye before he returned to his post at a cannon, where he died.

After the battle, when the survivors were discovered, they were taken to the governor's house and interrogated by Santa Anna himself. He was charmed by Angelina and wanted to adopt her, but Susanna refused. The general gave Susanna a silver peso and a blanket, and told her to inform Gen. Houston that death awaited all Texian traitors who defied him. He ordered the Texian bodies to be stacked into a large funeral pyre, layered with pieces of wood, and set ablaze. All the while Susanna told her story, Gen. Houston held her hand, and that old tough soldier wept like a little boy.

Afterwards, Susanna caught my eye and whispered, "Your brother and uncle died swiftly." When I asked her about Lem, she said she never saw him there the whole time she was in the Alamo.

As I ran home, Papa met me on the trail to the cabin and I sobbed in his arms for the longest time until I felt limp as a rag doll. He told me to wait under the tree while he broke the news to Mama. She saw him coming up the path and stood still. Papa removed his hat and his voice was all hoarse and shaky.

"Mrs. Lawrence, our son and your brother Isaac have given their lives for liberty." That's how Papa worded it. Mama crumpled to the porch and buried her face in her apron. The only other time I saw her sob like that was when Baby Mary died in her arms. Her whole body shook and shook. Papa sat beside her and put his arms around her and patted her shoulder.

Papa told me to go find Green so I went back to town looking for him. I found him curled inside an empty pork barrel crying. I held out my hand and he came into my arms like a little puppy lost in the rain.

Later —

I have never seen such misery as I saw in Gonzales tonight, and I pray I never see it again. Every house has lost someone, whether it be a father or brother, uncle or son. The wild shrieks of widows and fatherless children filled the air up and down the muddy streets. Out of thirty cabins, there are twenty widows for sure, maybe more.

As I led Green back home, the most awful confusion and panic began to stir in the streets. Gen. Houston's men hurried by — men on foot, men on horses, men in wagons. They were causing such a commotion that residents opened their doors and looked out windows.

"What's happening?" I asked Mrs. DeWitt as she scurried by.

"Santa Anna reached Sandy Creek last night by force marching his soldiers twenty-four miles a day. The Mexican army will be in Gonzales tomorrow," she said. "Gen. Houston has decided not to stay and fight. He has ordered a retreat. He counted his men and found we now have only three hundred and seventy-five, not enough to face the whole Mexican army."

About that time a door opened and a man shouted out to a passing group of Houston's men, "In the name of God, gentlemen, I hope you are not going to leave the families behind!"

Someone in the rank shouted back in a sarcastic voice, "Oh, yes. We are all looking out for Number One."

I grabbed Green's hand and ran like the dickens back to the house. I told Papa and he cursed Gen. Houston something fierce for retreating. Then he said he'd not allow his wagon and mules to be used by a fleeing army. He told us to pack while he went to get our wagon. Mama was still numb from the news about the Alamo.

"Mama, we've got to pack," I said, but she didn't move from the front porch. "Mama, the Mexicans are almost here."

She shook her head and looked up; her eyes were red and swollen.

"I'll not leave without Lemuel," she whispered. "You said Susanna did not see him at the Alamo."

I know I was a selfish ungrateful child, but I cried out, "Mama, we can't help Lemuel — he's gone. But you've still got two children who need you." That seemed to clear her stupor, for she rose, gave me and Green a hug and kiss, then started giving orders. I was never so glad to hear her telling me what to do.

We pulled everything of value from the house — there wasn't time to get the heavy furniture; it was mostly rough-hewn anyway. We packed our clothes in the same trunk that had made the trip from Missouri and buried it in soft sand in the woods. Mama made us put on our shoes, though the trails and fields are muddy. She decided to hide her spinning wheel in the barn loft.

Most of the widows have no wagons, and in spite

of what Papa said about Gen. Houston, I saw him ordering his men to turn over the army's wagons to the women who needed them the most. He told the troops to throw their two cannons into the Guadalupe River so the Mexicans wouldn't get them, as there is no way to haul heavy artillery in the retreat.

It is dark now, but the whole town is lit up from lanterns and candles. The lights would be beautiful, were it not for the sadness that hangs over every house. I hear Papa coming with the wagon. Good-bye, my dear, beautiful town. You will always be in my heart. I swear I will return someday.

Monday, March 14

We left Gonzales late last night under black rain clouds. Papa drove the wagon, following the trail of lanterns. Gen. Houston's retreating soldiers followed right behind us. We were too numb with grief to talk and I heard women and children weeping all around us as we trudged along all night, hoping to get a good lead on the Mexican army.

At daybreak we saw a brilliant red-orange glow in the west. It was Gonzales being burned to the ground by order of Gen. Houston. I won't repeat here what Papa had to say about the general.

Oh, my beautiful little town! All those years of toil, all the precious things we collected and treasured so dearly, all the furniture and houses we built with our own hands — everything reduced to ashes.

I cried, "Oh, Mama, your spinning wheel." A man standing nearby said, "Isn't it better it burns to the ground than let the Mexicans have it?" Then Papa said, "I never knew a spinning wheel to be used as a weapon of war."

I cannot stop thinking about Willis and his last moments on earth. I wonder if he fought hand to hand, or if a bullet brought him down. Did Uncle Isaac die first? Did their hearts tremble with fear? And what happened to Lem? If he comes home, what will he think? And that nice boy James Allen — how can I ever again kiss a boy and not think of him? And dear Galba — Oh, my head will not stop spinning with horrid images. I can write no more. My heart aches too much.

Tuesday, March 15

The mud is deep and wagons are bogged down everywhere. Our clothing is drenched and caked with mud. I wrapped my precious diary and Mama's Bible in a piece of cowhide and carry them in my arms. Too tired to write.

Wednesday, March 16

Gen. Houston sent some men back to get the blind Widow Millsaps and her seven children, though we have already traveled close to thirty miles. I think that was considerate of him. I have seen no sign of the Roes. I hope we catch up with their wagon. I want to talk to someone, but cannot bother Mama with my grief.

I have come to dread sleep, for nightmares haunt me all through the night. When I awake each morning I feel as if I have died a thousand deaths.

Thursday, March 17

Reached the Colorado River. Hundreds of settlers are here, waiting for the ferry to take them across a few at a time, as the river is high and raging. Some tried to cross but the strong current swept horses, wagons, and cattle away. Gen. Houston's army moved higher up the river, but we will cross here.

Many children have come down with a shaking fever. Their little bodies tremble and convulse. Some have died in their mothers' arms. Most all of us have sore throats from being in wet clothes night and day. Papa's leg is worse.

Friday, March 18

Cried all day, thinking about Willis, Uncle Isaac, and Galba. I still cannot believe they are gone. I keep asking myself, What did they die for? Nothing was gained; we have no free Texas; we are fleeing to the States like scared rabbits. Now I know why Papa hates war.

Saturday, March 19

Johnnie Kellog's young widow gave birth today. It was pouring rain, so she lay in the back of a cart and women held a blanket over her while she delivered. There are no men among us, except for the old or crippled and Negroes from the plantations. The roads and fields are strewn with abandoned furniture, tools, wagons, carts, and dead mules and oxen. Six years of toil sunk in the mud. The wolves and buzzards are fat from feasting.

Monday, March 21

We reached San Felipe settlement on the Brazos River and located Uncle Henry's cabin. Everything was abandoned, with soup still in the kettle. Aunt Nancy left a note saying they had gone east to Liberty, on the far side of the Trinity River, to stay with her brother's family. She wants us to join her. Mama's spirits lifted some to hear that Aunt Nancy is safe.

Papa cannot walk. We had to carry him from the wagon to the bed. We will rest a day or two here as there has been no word of Mexicans nearby. It feels so wonderful to sleep in a real bed. Green found a pup and clings to it like a babe clings to a doll.

Tuesday, March 22

The ferry runs night and day across the raging Brazos. I still cannot sleep. I keep imagining Willis and Galba in their dying moments. If I do not see Mittie again, I guess the story of my first kiss with James Allen will be my secret forever. When I close my eyes I still see his kind face.

Wednesday, March 23

One of our mules is dead. Papa said it was just worn out. There is not another mule, horse, or ox to be bought, even if we had the money to buy one. Since it takes two mules to pull the wagon, we will have to walk to Liberty. Papa cannot make the trip because of his leg, so he is staying here. He said he will hide in the woods if the Mexicans come and then make his way back to Gonzales when they are gone. He told us not to worry.

We hugged and kissed Papa good-bye and I thought our hearts would break. We are carrying only food, fresh water, the Bible, and my diary. San Felipe is to be burnt to the ground like Gonzales. Please, God, protect Papa.

Sunday, March 27

I have not written for days for I foolishly dropped my pencils into the Brazos River. Today Green found an ink bottle and quill in an abandoned cabin and gave them to me. Sometimes he can be so sweet.

I drank from a creek and now have the running trots. Have to stop behind bushes every half hour. I am too weak to stand, but there is no time to rest. Green feels poorly, too. He showed me his throat, swollen and fiery red, but he begged me not to tell Mama. At supper time, Green could not swallow his food. He has a fever. Mama said we will rest in the woods for a while. She held him close all night and rocked him, holding that hound pup. Poor Mama. Her big hips are bony now. Her face is tired and gray underneath the dirty bonnet.

Monday, March 28

Two men rode by. They told us that Col. Fannin surrendered all four hundred of his men to the Mexicans at Goliad on March 20. As the two men were leaving, a woman, who looked like she'd been half-eaten by a bear she was so wore out, fell to her knees in the road and begged the men to shoot her and put her out of her misery. Another woman did the same thing.

Mama got boiling mad and shouted, "You women should be ashamed! Didn't our husbands and sons and brothers just *die* for Texas? The least we can do is honor their memory and *live* for Texas." With those words she stomped through the mud holding herself like a queen. She didn't say a word about Uncle Henry, but we know he is doomed. Every Texian who has surrendered to Santa Anna so far has been murdered.

★ ★ ★

Tuesday, March 29

The peach orchards are aglow with pink blossoms and the prairies are blanketed with beautiful flowers, so spring has arrived. But in my heart it is still the deepest, darkest winter.

Wednesday, March 30

Reached the San Jacinto River today, the third river we have come to. Seething crowds gather at Lynchberg Ferry, some say five thousand. Many of them are Negroes from the big plantations. The ferry-man is allowing those with sick children to go first.

There are epidemics of measles, dysentery, and whooping cough. Some say there is cholera, too. I saw a tiny grave with the name "Permelia Roe" scratched on a stone — Mittie's little sister.

We did not get across today. Will have to sleep in the mud tonight, but it does not matter anymore. We are the most miserable lot you've ever seen.

April

I do not know the date anymore. I contracted sore eyes while we waited three days for the ferry. My eyes swelled shut; I could not see to read or write, nor even to walk. Green and Mama took turns holding my hand. We caught up with a cart that had some leather straps attached to the back. The driver told me I could hold on to the straps for guidance. How I hated not knowing what my feet would step into next, or what snake or alligator or other creature might sink its fangs into my ankles. I am blind in my left eye now, but I have regained good vision in my right.

Another April day

We have reached our fourth river, the Trinity. On the other side will be Aunt Nancy, a soft bed, dry clothes, and food waiting for us. But the Trinity has overflown her banks and is ten miles wide. Of all the rivers and creeks we have crossed, this one is by far the worst. Some of the families have decided to stay here on this side and take their chances with Santa Anna, rather than cross that river. Mama says we will wait one or two days to see if the water goes down. It is dark now and I write by the light of a campfire. I can see the lights of Liberty far away in the distance, but they might as well be on the moon.

★ ★ ★

April, day unknown

The water is still rising. Mama is torn with indecision. She wants to join Aunt Nancy, but crossing the Trinity is too dangerous.

The next day

A courier rode up. He told us all four hundred men at Goliad were massacred on Palm Sunday — taken out to the road and shot down unarmed.

Mama let out a little gasp and squeezed my hand until it hurt, then she thanked the man. She didn't cry; I think we already knew Uncle Henry had been lost. Mama just said, "What am I going to tell Nancy?"

The messenger also brought word that Santa Anna has crossed the Brazos and is headed for Harrisburg, the town near the San Jacinto River where the government of the Republic of Texas was located when we passed through. Like us, the new government is trying to keep one step ahead of the Mexican army. No word on Houston's army.

★ ★ ★

Three days later

At last we crossed the raging Trinity River. Floating logs and debris bombarded the side of the flatboat causing it to rock and teeter. It took eight strong men to navigate. It was the most frightening experience.

We located Aunt Nancy at her brother's house in Liberty. She and Mama hugged and cried. Aunt Nancy pulled her children close and told them their father had gone to Heaven. I could not help but think of my own dear papa and wonder if he had escaped Santa Anna's troops. And what of Aunt Esperanza and Baby Wash? What would become of them without Uncle Isaac? And what happened to dear Lemuel?

One more April day

Today we met a man from Nacogdoches who was looking for Houston and the Texian army so he might join, but no one knows where the general is. The stranger said he had met a man named Louis Rose, who claimed to have escaped from the Alamo. Mr. Rose said on the last night before the fall, Col. Travis assembled the men, then drew a line in the sand with his sword and gave them the choice to stay and face death, or to slip away in the night. Only Mr. Rose did not step forward, and only Mr. Rose survived.

Now, when I close my eyes at night, I see Willis stepping across that line, head high and shoulders squared. Unlike the time he stepped over old Ben Milam's line all those months ago, this time he must have known he would die. All of them must have known. Oh, why, why did those Texians have to start this scrape! Were we so bad off to justify all this misery and losing those dear lives? I am too weary to think anymore. I have decided never to write again, for all I have is sad tidings.

Thursday, April 21

I have taken up my pen again for the news is urgent. This afternoon we heard a sudden noise in the west that sounded like distant thunder, but an old man who had fought in the War of 1812 said it was cannons. The cannonade lasted about fifteen minutes. The man shook his head and said, "It doesn't look very good, ladies. That's the end of Gen. Houston and the Texas army. Time to move on."

★ ★ ★

Friday, April 22

All hope has washed out of my soul. We packed all day and set out for the Sabine River, which is the border between Texas and the United States. Santa Anna dares not cross that river. Aunt Nancy, her sister-in-law, the children, and Mama rode in a sturdy covered wagon pulled by three yoke of oxen. Green and I rode on horses with two Negroes. Again we go into the darkness.

Saturday, April 23

I will never, ever forget this day! We had traveled a few miles and camped for the evening, when suddenly there was a loud ruckus. A man rode toward us furiously, waving his hat and shouting. We thought the Mexicans were upon us and jumped up to hitch the oxen. When he got closer, he yelled, "Turn back! Turn back! The Mexicans are defeated! It's safe to go back home!" He was a colorful man with an Irish brogue. "The Texians charged the Mexican troops while they were having an afternoon siesta. Our boys shouted, 'Remember the Alamo! Remember Goliad!' and their ardor won the victory. Santa Anna was in his silken tent with a woman. He tried to escape dressed like a private, but was caught. No one would have known who he was, except his men all whispered *El Presidente* whenever he walked by *and* his shirt had diamond studs!"

I never heard such whooping and yelling in all my born days. Women and children, Negroes, and returning men all put up such a scene it looked like a Methodist revival meeting. They are still celebrating.

Sunday, April 24

Early this morning the Roe wagon passed by. I was so happy I nearly cried when I saw Mittie, but she was quiet and sad. Her dress was ripped and filthy; her feet were bare; her hair ribbon was in shreds.

"Mama says we're going back to Missoura," Mittie said. Mrs. Roe had lost another child, her little boy, along the way and was very peaked-looking.

Mama said, "Why, Sarah Roe, surely you ain't going to abandon your home in Gonzales. Who'll watch over your petunias?"

Mrs. Roe forced a weak smile and said, "You can have the petunias and the Indians and the Mexicans and the mosquitoes and alligators, Rebecca. You can have all of Texas. I've had enough."

I said good-bye to Mittie and it truly hurt. She was

crying as she sat in the back of the wagon, waving good-bye.

Mama climbed back into Aunt Nancy's wagon and we turned around toward the west, toward home. "Are we going back to Missoura?" Green asked.

"No, sir," Mama said. "We've put too much blood and tears in this Texas soil to turn back now. And I know your papa and Lemuel and Esperanza and Baby Wash are still alive. I have a premonition in my heart."

Green and I smiled at each other. We knew that Mama's premonitions were always right.

Epilogue
★ ★ ★

The return trip to Gonzales took over a month and was almost as treacherous as the "Runaway Scrape," as the fleeing of the settlers came to be called. When the weary Lawrence family arrived back at Gonzales, they found their log cabin partially burned, but Papa and Lem were waiting with open arms, and the cotton, corn, and vegetables were up and healthy. Lem had been captured by Comanche on his way to fight at the Alamo, and did not escape until many weeks later. He credited his pet crow with leading him back home.

Lemuel Lawrence became a doctor, specializing in the science of animal care. He married a farm girl and raised eight children, two of whom became veterinarians.

Green Lawrence was bitten by "gold fever" in 1849 and moved to California where he did not strike it rich. But he met and married a girl named Mollie who made a small fortune cooking and washing and selling goods to the miners.

Aunt Esperanza returned to San Antonio and remarried. Wash grew tall and burly like his father. He drove cattle along the famous Chisolm Trail and later bought a ranch in Bexar County. His descendants still live there today.

Mittie Roe stayed in Missouri, but wrote Lucinda often. She married a wealthy clothing merchant and had all the dresses and hair ribbons she wanted. She named her first child after her best friend.

Lucinda Lawrence continued to read books and to educate herself. She attended San Augustine Female Academy, then moved to the newly founded town called Houston and became a teacher. She married the son of a well-to-do farmer in Fort Bend. During the Civil War, Lucinda's husband and oldest son fought with Terry's Rangers and both were killed. She moved to Galveston Island where her youngest son prospered in the shipping business. He built a mansion, which was destroyed by the Great Hurricane of 1900. Lucinda returned to her beloved Gonzales, where she spent the rest of her days in a simple house on Water Street. She lived to be eighty-three years old.

Life in America
in 1836

Historical Note

★ ★ ★

Spanish explorers first saw Texas in 1519. They named the region "Tejas," the Indian word for friend. The Spanish mostly ignored the vast region for the next one hundred and fifty years. In 1685, explorer Robert LaSalle landed in Texas and claimed it for France. Word of LaSalle's fort made Spain realize the need for strengthening its claim to Texas. Between 1690 and 1793, Spain established thirty-six missions in Texas for the purpose of converting native Indians to the Catholic religion, to establish Spanish settlements, and to thwart French claims.

Mission San Antonio de Valero (later known as the Alamo) was one of several missions built near the San Antonio River. Established in 1718, the Valero mission was abandoned by the padres and friars around 1790. From 1801–1825, the mission was occupied by Spanish soldiers and converted into a fort. During this time it became known as the Alamo, the Spanish word for cottonwood tree. San Antonio de Bexar, the settlement that grew up around the missions in this area, became the largest Spanish town in Texas.

In 1821, Mexico declared her independence from Spain and a young general, Antonio López de Santa Anna, emerged as a Mexican war hero.

The new Republic of Mexico agreed to allow Americans to colonize Texas, mainly as a buffer zone between Mexican settlements and Indian raids. Men who received permission from the Mexican government to bring families to Texas were called *empresarios.* Stephen F. Austin was the first *empresario* to lead American families to Texas. Austin's Colony, whose main settlement was San Felipe de Austin on the Brazos River, was the largest. The second largest colony was established by *empresario* Green DeWitt, and its main town was Gonzales, on the Guadalupe River.

The colonists had several stringent criteria to pass: They had to be of high moral character; they had to agree to become Mexican citizens and obey Mexico's constitution; they had to become Catholics; they had to settle the land within a limited time period. In exchange they received large land grants and were exempt from taxes and duties for several years. A colony consisted of farmers and ranchers spread out over hundreds of square miles, and also small towns. The towns contained merchant shops, blacksmith shops, doctors, lawyers, and supply stores. Early settlers had no schools or churches.

The Texians quickly built homes out of logs and planted corn, their main food. Wealthy planters brought slaves with them and established successful cotton plantations. Isolated from the United States and from Mexico City, these Texians flourished and became self-sufficient. They made their own clothes, furniture, soap, candles, and tools. They ate venison, wild fowl, or domestic pigs for meat. They captured wild mustangs that roamed the countryside in great herds, as well as longhorn cattle that likewise roamed free. They rarely saw Mexican officials or a Catholic priest. Most did not speak Spanish and did not trade or associate with the Mexican citizens of Texas, the Tejanos. They remained American in beliefs and actions.

For several years, Americans flooded into Texas, including thousands of illegal squatters. By 1830, there were over thirty thousand English-speaking Texians, five thousand slaves, and only four thousand Spanish-speaking Tejanos, living mostly in San Antonio de Bexar. Alarmed by this, the Mexican government passed the Law of 1830 prohibiting further immigration of Americans. This caused great resentment among the Texians.

General Santa Anna was elected President of Mexico

in 1833. He believed in a dictatorial form of government, and gradually began taking away the power of the individual states in the Republic. He abolished the Constitution of 1824, levied taxes and duties, and sent soldiers to Texas. Texians had no representation in the Mexican government and the state capital was hundreds of miles away in Coahuila.

Texians held conventions to discuss action. In 1833, Stephen F. Austin took a list of grievances to Mexico City. He was arrested and jailed, contracting a lung disease while there. After being released in 1835, he no longer believed that a peaceful solution was possible.

By 1835, the unrest had grown, and several clashes occurred between Texians and Mexican soldiers. When Santa Anna garrisoned soldiers in the Alamo, Texians expected the worst and called to Americans for help.

In the States, Volunteers formed companies to fight for Texas in exchange for free land. Most of the Volunteers were young adventurers looking for a fight and the spoils of war. The first battle of the war occurred in tiny Gonzales, when Mexican soldiers tried to take back a small cannon given to the colonists for protection from the Indians. The Texians refused to give it up, unfurling a white flag that read, "Come and Take It."

Hundreds of Volunteers flocked to Texas to take

part in the war. Some Tejanos joined the Texian cause also. In December 1835, a band of Texians, Tejanos, and Volunteers from the States drove the Mexican soldiers from the Alamo in the Battle of Bexar.

Most of the Texians, whose farms needed working, returned home. That left only one hundred and fifty men at San Antonio to fortify and defend the Alamo. No one worried about General Santa Anna because it was winter, the wrong time of year to move armies. But a furious Santa Anna gathered six thousand soldiers, artillery, and supplies, and force marched them across the Mexican desert and mountains into Texas. Many soldiers were green conscripts from tropical Mexico who had never experienced cold weather and who were wearing thin cotton clothing and no shoes. Hit by a severe blizzard, several hundred soldiers died from hunger and exposure, as did many pack animals.

Santa Anna's advance guard arrived in San Antonio on February 23, 1836, much to the surprise of the Texians, who had just celebrated George Washington's birthday with a lively fandango. They hurriedly secured themselves inside the Alamo, along with several Tejanos, and a few women and children.

The siege lasted thirteen days, with no Texian casualties until the final assault on March 6. In spite of several heartfelt pleas for help from William Travis, the twenty-six-year-old commander, only thirty-two men came to his aid, all from tiny Gonzales. According to some historians, Travis drew a line in the sand with his sword on their final night and gave the men the opportunity to stay and face death or to leave. Only one man, Louis Moses Rose, an experienced Napoleonic soldier, refused to step over the line.

Word of the fall of the Alamo reached the settlements by way of Susanna Dickinson. She, her baby girl, and Joe, the black servant of Travis's, were the only Americans to survive the battle. Young James Allen narrowly escaped because Travis chose him to be the last messenger to deliver a final desperate plea to Colonel Fannin in Goliad.

Learning that the Mexican army was marching toward the settlements, the colonists fled east toward the United States in the "Runaway Scrape." Having only three hundred and seventy-five men in the Texas army, General Sam Houston ordered a retreat. As the worst rains in memory thrashed the fleeing settlers, the women and children endured deplorable conditions. Swollen rivers carried off wagons, horses, and people. Bad water caused dysentery and typhoid. Diseases such as whooping cough, measles, and pneumonia killed many children. Close behind the fleeing settlers, Santa Anna's army steadily marched eastward.

Near the small town of Goliad, south of Gonzales, Mexicans captured about four hundred Texians and Volunteers. On Palm Sunday, March 27, the unarmed prisoners were massacred. Houston continued his retreat, waiting for the right time to attack, much to the disgruntlement of many settlers. Santa Anna split his forces, and on April 21, 1836, near the San Jacinto River, Houston finally made a bold daytime attack, and defeated the Mexican troops to the shouts of "Remember the Alamo! Remember Goliad!" Santa Anna, who escaped by dressing as a private, was captured and forced to sign a treaty recognizing Texas independence. Santa Anna returned to Mexico where he was ousted, but returned to power several more times during his lifetime.

The Republic of Texas flourished between 1836 and 1845, and thousands of Americans and Europeans immigrated there. Texas joined the Union in December 1845, becoming the twenty-eighth state. Soon, the Mexican War erupted between the United States and Mexico. General Santa Anna led Mexican forces once again, but was defeated. In 1847, Mexico ceded California and its other lands, opening up what became the American West.

Texan girls wore long dresses while they performed household tasks. On special occasions, they dressed in fancier gowns with a petticoat underneath. Bonnets were worn with all different clothes.

Women and girls worked hard all day long. Farm life required them to make their own soap. Fat from slaughtered farm animals was boiled in a large iron pot over a fire and mixed with lye, an alkaline substance made from ashes and water. The mixture was then poured into molds, where it gradually thickened into soap. Although effective for cleansing, lye soap was very harsh on the skin.

For enjoyment, Texans (who called themselves Texians long ago) gathered together for fandangos, or dances, to listen to lively music and socialize. These celebrations were often quite rowdy and would last late into the night.

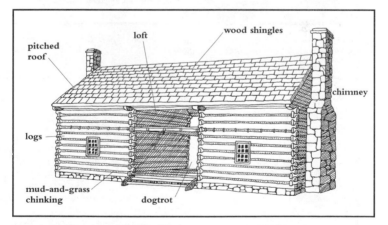

Prior to the 1800s, the Spanish and Mexican population had built mostly primitive adobe houses in Texas. With the introduction of log houses by the Anglo Americans, a new architectural style began to develop in Texas. Log houses often consisted of two rooms, with a "dog trot," or open hall, between them, and an attic space used for sleeping. Doors from each room connected to the "dog trot," making it a useful area for hanging wash on rainy days, storing meat in the winter, and relaxing on hot days.

191

Mexican girls and women dressed in long ruffled skirts. Many skirts were woven with vibrant colors and worn with ruffled petticoats.

This typical hacienda on a Mexican ranch in the 1800s was built on one level and made of wood, adobe, and tile. Three wings arranged in a "u" provided shade for a garden or patio. A veranda, or roofed porch, ran along each wing. All rooms opened onto the veranda, which provided a cool place for outdoor living.

The war for Texan independence began when Mexican soldiers came to take the six pounder cannon from Texans at Gonzales. The Texans refused, flying a flag that said, "Come and take it." The Texan volunteers wore ragged buckskins and used rifles to defend themselves.

The Mexican army wore uniforms in dark blue and white with leather hats, or plain white fatigues. Several thousand in number, they were equipped with many cannons, and had well-trained military leadership.

This ad, issued in New Orleans before the news of the defeat at the Alamo, offered free land to inhabitants of the United States willing to volunteer to fight for the independence of Texas. Ads often spoke harshly against Mexicans, who were considered the Texans' "enemy." However, many Mexican Texans, called Tejanos, fought bravely against Santa Anna and his soldiers.

Forty-six days after the battle at the Alamo, Sam Houston led a small group of Americans in combat, surprised the Mexican troops, and captured Santa Anna, who was forced to sign a treaty declaring Texas an independent state. In 1836, Houston was elected the first president of Texas.

At the battle of the Alamo on March 6, 1836, fewer than two hundred Texans attempted to defend the old mission. Spanning over three acres, it proved too expansive to secure, and the Texans were overcome and brutally defeated by the Mexican army. All of the rebel soldiers were killed in less than two hours, and over six hundred Mexicans died as well.

The Alamo was founded in 1718 by Spanish padres as the Mission San Antonio de Valero. This earliest photograph of the Alamo (as it appeared in the 1850s) shows the Long Barracks at the left, where the padres lived. The "hump" on the church was not built until 1847, many years after the battle of the Alamo. Today the Long Barracks serves as a museum, and the Alamo chapel is referred to as "The Shrine of Texas Liberty."

195

In 1833, Antonio López de Santa Anna took control of Mexico. A former politician and soldier in the Spanish army, Santa Anna was a skilled and ruthless leader. During his rule as president, he eliminated the Mexican Constitution of 1824 (similar to the U.S. constitution) and acted as dictator. Texans lost their political voice and even those loyal to Mexico (known as Peace Party members) opposed Santa Anna's dictatorship.

Susanna Dickinson was a real person who, with her baby daughter, Angelina, survived the battle of the Alamo, as did twelve others, mostly Mexican women and children. Her husband, Captain Almeron Dickinson, a member of the rebel army, was killed in the battle.

TURKEY IN THE STRAW

With a lively beat

Traditional Square Dance Tune

1. As I was goin' down the road with a tired team and a heavy load, I cracked my whip and the leader sprung, I says day-hay to the wagon tongue.

Chorus

Tur-key in the straw, tur-key in the hay, Tur-key in the straw, tur-key in the hay, Roll 'em up and twist 'em up a

1. As I was goin' down the road with
   a tired team and a heavy load, I
   cracked my whip and the leader
   sprung, I says hay to the wagon
   tongue.

   Chorus
   Turkey in the straw, turkey in the
   hay, Turkey in the straw, turkey in
   the hay. Roll 'em up and twist
   'em up a high tuck-a-haw, And
   hit 'em up a tune called Turkey
   in the Straw.

2. Oh, I went out to milk, and I
   didn't know how; I milked a goat
   instead of a cow. A monkey sittin'
   on a pile of straw. A-winkin' his
   eye at his mother-in-law.

   Chorus
   Turkey in the straw, turkey in the
   hay, Turkey in the straw, turkey in
   the hay. Roll 'em up and twist
   'em up a high tuck-a-haw, And
   hit 'em up a tune called Turkey
   in the Straw.

"Turkey in the Straw" was a popular song in Texas in 1836, and was often played on the fiddle.

Modern map of the United States showing the approximate location of Gonzales, Texas.

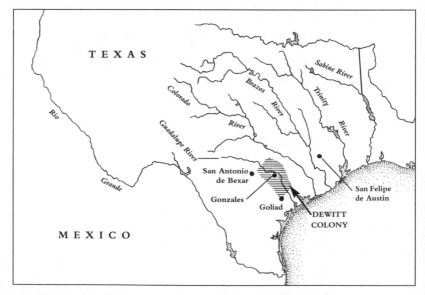

This map shows the cities and rivers that played an important role in Texas history in 1836.

About the Author

★ ★ ★

A fifth generation Texan whose great-great grand-father went to Texas while it was still a Republic, SHERRY GARLAND has always been proud of her heritage and the unique history of the Lone Star State. "As a child living in a small town, I attended William B. Travis Elementary School," she says. "Each morning as I entered the redbrick building, I would pause and look at the large painting that depicted William Travis drawing a line in the sand in front of the Alamo chapel. That scene stuck in my mind, and I've always had a fascination with the heroes of the Battle of the Alamo.

"As a teenager, I attended Sam Houston High School. One of the most fortunate events of my life occurred when my English teacher made the entire class enter an essay writing contest. The name of the contest was 'Why I Love Texas.' Having lived mostly on farms and in small towns, my traveling experiences were limited, so I began my essay with these words,

'I've never seen the Alamo; I've never seen San Jacinto. . . .' Because of this, friends and relatives teased me endlessly, and always ended notes and letters with the words, 'Hope you get to see the Alamo.' I won that essay contest and with that began my interest in a writing career. So I've always had a love for those hallowed walls.

"I was almost thirty when I finally saw the Alamo for the first time. I was awed by the thick white walls and the feeling of history that surrounded me. I have returned many times since then and am always moved by the tragedy that occurred there.

"The opportunity to present a fictitious girl, living at the time of the Texas Revolution was both challenging and rewarding. I gave the girl, Lucinda Lawrence, my great-grandmother's maiden name. I wanted Lucinda to be an ordinary girl, caught up in the war, the tragedies of the Alamo and Goliad, the horror of the Runaway Scrape, and the final victory at San Jacinto. After researching the history of Texas, I now know that the history books I studied from as a child were not totally truthful. The men who participated in the Texas Revolution were not perfect. Some of them were downright scoundrels. The causes of the war were far more complicated than a fight for freedom. And the Mexican government had just cause for fighting, too. But in the end, those men who fought at the Alamo died heroes, for they faced sure death with bravery and courage."

Sherry Garland is the critically acclaimed author of twenty-five books for children, young adults, and adults. She has received numerous awards and honors, including the Texas Institute of Letters Award, the California Young Readers Medal, and the Western Writers of America Spur Award. Among her well-known novels are *Song of the Buffalo Boy, Shadow of the Dragon,* and *Indio,* all ALA Best Books for Young Adults. She and her husband live in Houston, Texas.

In honor of my great-great-grandparents,
Andrew Jackson Long and
Mittie Roe Long,
whose pioneering spirit brought them
to the Republic of Texas,
and in loving memory
of Desla Camp Allison.

Acknowledgments
★ ★ ★

My deepest appreciation goes to Dr. Richard Bruce Winders, Curator at the Alamo, for checking the manuscript for historical accuracy.

★ ★ ★

Grateful acknowledgmenmt is made for permission to reprint the following:

Cover portrait: *The Girl at the Gate* by George Clause, 1889. Oil on canvas. Courtesy of the Tate Gallery, London/Art Resources, New York.

Cover background: *Dawn at the Alamo* by Henry A. McCardle, 1905. Courtesy of the Texas State Library and Archives Commission, Austin, Texas.

Page 190 (top): Texan girl, drawing by Heather Saunders
Page 190 (bottom): Soapmaking, Brown Brothers, Sterling, Pennsylvania.
Page 191 (top): Dancing at Saloon, Library of Congress
Page 191 (bottom): Dogtrot Cabin, drawing by Heather Saunders
Page 192 (top): Mexican women. lithograph by Carlos Nebel, published in 1836, New York Public Library Picture Collection, New York, New York.
Page 192 (bottom): Hacienda, North Wind Picture Archives, Alfred, Maine.
Page 193 (top): Texan soldiers, Osprey Publishing, London, England.
Page 193 (bottom): Mexican soldiers, ibid.

Page 194 (top): Texas Forever, Broadsides Collection, The Center for
American History, The University of Texas at Austin,
Austin, Texas.

Page 194 (bottom): Sam Houston, Library of Congress

Page 195 (top): Alamo lithograph, Library of Congress

Page 195 (bottom): Alamo Church and Plaza, Daughters of the Republic
of Texas Library at the Alamo, San Antonio, Texas

Page 196 (top): Daguerreotype of Santa Anna, Collection of San Jacinto
Museum of History, San Antonio, Texas.

Page 196 (bottom): Susanna Dickinson, Prints and Photographs Collection,
The Center for American History, The University of Texas at
Austin, Austin, Texas.

Page 197: "Turkey in the Straw," Traditional, arrangement by Denes Agay.

Page 198: Maps by Heather Saunders

Other books in the Dear America series

★ ★ ★

A Journey to the New World
The Diary of Remember Patience Whipple
by Kathryn Lasky

The Winter of Red Snow
The Revolutionary War Diary of Abigail Jane Stewart
by Kristiana Gregory

When Will This Cruel War Be Over?
The Civil War Diary of Emma Simpson
by Barry Denenberg

A Picture of Freedom
The Diary of Clotee, a Slave Girl
by Patricia C. McKissack

Across the Wide and Lonesome Prairie
The Oregon Trail Diary of Hattie Campbell
by Kristiana Gregory

So Far From Home
The Diary of Mary Driscoll, an Irish Mill Girl
by Barry Denenberg

I Thought My Soul Would Rise and Fly
The Diary of Patsy, a Freed Girl
by Joyce Hansen

West to a Land of Plenty
The Diary of Teresa Angelino Viscardi
by Jim Murphy

Dreams in the Golden Country
The Diary of Zipporah Feldman, a Jewish Immigrant Girl
by Kathryn Lasky

Standing in the Light
The Captive Diary of Catharine Carey Logan
by Mary Pope Osborne

Voyage on the Great Titanic
The Diary of Margaret Ann Brady
by Ellen Emerson White

Copyright © 1998 by Sherry Garland.

★　★　★

All rights reserved. Published by Scholastic Inc. DEAR AMERICA and the
DEAR AMERICA logo
are trademarks of Scholastic Inc.

Library of Congress Cataloging-in-Publication Data
Garland, Sherry.
A line in the sand: the Alamo diary of Lucinda Lawrence
by Sherry Garland.
p. cm. — (Dear America; 11)
Summary: In the diary she receives for her thirteenth birthday in 1835,
Lucinda Lawrence describes the hardships her family and other residents of the
"Texas colonies" endure when they decide to face the Mexicans in a fight for
their freedom.
ISBN 0-590-39466-5 (alk. paper)
1. Texas — History — Revolution 1835–1836 — Juvenile fiction.
[1. Texas — History — Revolution 1835–1836 — Juvenile fiction.
2. Frontier and pioneer life — Fiction. 3. Family life —Texas — Fiction.
4. Diaries — Fiction.] I. Title. II. Series.
PZ7.G18415Li 1998
[Fic] — dc2   LC #:97-40638
CIP   AC
10   9   8   7   6   5   4   3   2   1   8   9/9   0/0   01   02   03

The display type was set in Chanson D'Amour
The text type was set in Bembo
Book design by Elizabeth B. Parisi

Printed in the U.S.A.
First printing, September 1998

★　★　★